KEEPING MY DRAC

A Dragon's Peak Novella

MEGAN LANDON

MEGAN LANDON

For Melissa S.

My first reader. Thank you, my beautiful friend.

CONTENTS

1

A New Moon

Arik

On the new moon, I descend on silent wings, swift like an owl. The shadows of the palace's garden terraces conceal me as I shift into human form. Appearing clad in black leather pants and tunic, I drop to the ground under the cover of darkness and await my treasure.

Ophelia hides in the shadows, and I smile. She believes herself stealthy, but my drac vision gives me the advantage over her human senses in the dark. She breaks from her shady cover and runs toward me, her black cloak billowing around her.

"Arik," she whispers as she leaps toward me. Ready, I catch her midair and enfold her in my arms as she wraps her legs around my waist.

"Princess," I whisper before our mouths come together in a hungry kiss.

Her cloak opens to reveal perfect, plump breasts. Naked. My heart almost stops in my chest. My feisty, adventurous princess, always full of sweet surprises.

"Ophelia," I moan and lift her to kiss one puckered nipple. "You can't be running around naked."

"I'm covered, and there's no one around."

"Your guards are worthless. And you'll catch your death of cold."

"I'm stealthy." She laughs as I pull her against me. "And you keep me warm."

"I know where I can keep you warm." A trusting smile curves her lip as she wraps both her arms around one of mine, readying herself for my shift. After two years, my intrepid love anticipates all my maneuvers, though I do like surprising her, as she does me.

In two running steps, I leap into the air, shifting into my dragon form and shifting her to cradle her in my foreclaws. My fearless princess loves to fly.

Staying close to the palace walls and low to the ground to avoid being seen, I coast over white sands until we're over the sea. I bank north to skirt the villages before circling around to the foothills and higher. As we soar, she strokes the underside of my neck, confident in my grip.

We reach the outcropping of boulders surrounded by a thick copse of trees. In the center is a steaming crystalline pool that melds with churning waters beneath a waterfall.

Settling her on her feet, I make to shift, but she stops me.

"Not yet," she says. "Let me look at you."

My black-and-dark-blue scales are iridescent, but I'm not sure how much she can see in the moonless night. So occupied admiring me, she ignores the beauty of the springs behind her.

I transform my face just enough to articulate a gentle command. "Take off your robe."

Her coy little smile makes my cock twinge as she opens her cloak to expose her luscious body. She slides the winter cloak lined with lambswool off her shoulders and catches it before it falls to the ground. My large body gives off enough heat that Ophelia need only stand by my side to stay comfortable and safe, despite the cold winter night.

Her body is graceful, her round ass swinging as she walks to a nearby boulder where she drapes her cloak. When she returns, her nipples hardening and her skin flushing in the crisp air, she hurries back to my warmth.

She caresses my muzzle with both hands and kisses the tip of my snout. I scent her wet need and lower my head to smell her cunt. She laughs and pushes my head away before running her hands along one side of my immense body. She rubs her naked breasts against my shoulder and, though my hide is tough, I sense each sumptuous point of contact on my flesh. Her delicate hands stroke my neck as she glides her body slowly against me. She gasps softly at the sensation of my warm, smooth scales against the tight buds of her nipples. She presses her lips against the corner of my mouth, unconcerned by sharp teeth.

I pick her up, fly her over the deep pool where the warm waters of the spring meet the falling waters of the icy mountain stream, and drop her. She squeals all the way down until she splashes into the warm water.

Ophelia

Laughing, I break through the water's surface. I plot my revenge as I swim toward the edge of the pool until an enormous splash sends a wall of water over me. Having dropped in his dragon form, my drac prince emerges as a man—a large, muscular, imposing man—set on catching me. I kick hard for the pool's edge.

Arik dives underwater, and a thrill shoots through me. My heart races, remembering my earlier anticipation of waiting naked in the dark and the thrill of watching him transform and stalk to me like a predator.

When a hand grips my ankle under the water, my racing heart settles into a pounding rhythm. He has me. Spinning, I catch him in return and wrap my arms and legs around him.

Arik breaks through the surface with me clinging to him like an octopus and carries me to the pool's edge, where the water near the spring is the hottest. He lifts me out of the water and onto the flat rock that's become a regular perch for our lovemaking. I lie back on the smooth stone, the intense contrast of the cold against my heated skin heightening my senses. My pounding heart stutters, and all the heat in my body surges to meet his mouth when he spreads my thighs and presses his face to my cunt.

The aching need I've felt all night—doused only for a moment during my unexpected plunge into the water—spikes with a voracity even Arik may not be able to slake.

"I've missed your taste," he says as he spreads my folds, exposing my wet pussy to the cool air. He licks me with his hot tongue, causing me to shiver again. After another decadent stroke, he pauses his ministrations to ask, "Have you missed me?"

"You know I have," I say, grinding myself shamelessly against his mouth.

"I've been dreaming about you," he moans against me as he slides two fingers inside my channel.

I grip his hair with both hands as I raise my knees to rest my feet on the rocky ledge, opening wide for him. The hunger in my core becomes so acute that my body tightens in response.

"That's it. Take your pleasure, my filthy princess."

He's incessant, tonguing my clit while drilling two thick fingers into me at a steady pace. When my pussy tightens around his fingers, he thrusts with the practiced urgency that feeds my hunger.

"Let go," he whispers, his hot breath fanning over my drenched pussy.

I surrender, pleasure hitting me like high tide in a hurricane. Waves of ecstasy wash through me as he stands between my legs and drives his cock into my slick heat in one exquisite thrust. I pull my knees toward my shoulders and take him as I ride out my orgasm, my cunt pulsing around his cock.

He plunges into me with a brutality I welcome. Later, our lovemaking will be slow. For now, he needs this. My cunt. My body. Me.

He glides his hands up my belly as his fucking becomes faster. He grips one breast roughly and squeezes my nipple. His other hand slides to the base of my throat. He presses firmly on my chest over my collarbones, holding me down as he pounds into me. His strong hand, possessive and dominating, sends a needy flutter through my body. I surrender to his power, and I'm rewarded when my body is whelmed by surging bliss.

"Again," he commands. "Again. Cum all over my cock."

Before the waves of my first orgasm have subsided, I feel myself tightening, ready to release again. He slips his hand between us and presses my clit with his thumb. My core pulses. I'm so close. He rubs a circle around my clit and presses again. He repeats the cycle rhythmically.

"Cum," he orders, and I let go again, welcoming the glorious waves washing through my body and crashing against the walls of my pussy to grip his cock.

He bucks spasmodically until he finally releases into me. I hold my arms open, and when he's spent, he falls against me. Wrapping my arms and legs around his big body, I hold him tight. He kisses my breasts, nibbling on the undersides, licking at my nipples.

"I love you," he whispers.

As waves of pleasure pulse through my body, I acknowledge his words with a moan. There will be time for sweet whispers later. For now, his weight comforts me as he nuzzles my breasts and runs his hands over my sides and ass.

Arik

I slide out of Ophelia's slick heat and lift her off the rock. Holding her to me, I lower us into the shallow water. She leans back with her legs wrapped around me, allowing the warm water to swirl around and between us. Her generous, pink-tipped breasts float at the surface of the water. I thumb one nipple as I meet my lips to hers.

Unable to keep my hands off Ophelia's enticing body, I slide one hand between us and stroke her folds lazily with the back of my finger. Even in the water, her honey and berries musk scent calls to me, urging me to claim her. My mate.

"You're going to tease me all night, aren't you?" she asks.

"Yes." I can't help smiling against her mouth. "I miss you. I want to talk. Surely, you don't simply want me for my body."

She reaches down and wraps her fingers around my cock. "At this precise moment, yes. Yes, I just want your body."

"Slattern."

She laughs. "Yes. That's me."

I lick the seam of her lips until she opens for me. We lose ourselves in the pleasure of exploring each other's taste. In the sensation of our mouths licking, sucking, and biting.

"Since we're talking," she says, breaking our kiss. "I want to ask you something."

She bites her lip. We've been sneaking away like this for more than a year, yet her shy smile makes her look like a girl learning how to let a boy know she likes him. I stroke a nipple as she speaks.

"The Spring Feast is a festival we celebrate when the season turns. I want you to come."

"The Spring Feast. That's your celebration of lovers, isn't it?"

"Yes. But it also celebrates all new beginnings. New babies. New planting season. New marriages. It's a long-held tradition in spring to bless new beginnings. Promises are made between young people, and often families are joined. This year my sisters are planning a masquerade."

"Dracs have the same celebration," I tell her. "We call it Fest de Verd in our language. It's when we also celebrate all the dragon matings for the year."

"Matings?"

"We don't have weddings. Dracs find their mate and they claim each other. Mated pairs are bound until death." I run my thumb over her plump bottom lip, the impulse to tell her she's my mate, my other half, poised on my own lips. "It's private between couples. But once a year we celebrate all the matings during our own Fest de Verd, our celebration of spring."

"As princess, I cannot attend the feast with a suitor. It's like Fest de..." She stumbles over the word.

"Fest de Verd," I say.

"Fest de Verd," she repeats, an excellent student of the drac language. "It would imply a promise of betrothal. But if you come, I'll save my dances for the handsome, masked stranger."

"I don't need a mask to dance with you." *You're my mate,* I want to tell her. She smiles and kisses me.

"If I went as your personal guest, and your people believed us betrothed, what would be so wrong with that?"

"Are you prepared to reveal yourself? Are dragon keepers, dracs, prepared to form an alliance? You're the drac chieftain's son. I'm a princess. We could form an alliance."

She says this playfully. She will be queen one day. She would never abandon her people. The truth drives a dagger into my chest, although it's comforting we share the same fantasy.

"You are one of the few humans aware of our existence, that we are both folk and dragon..." I let the thought dissipate with the steam around us. We only fantasize for so long before reality casts a shadow over our stolen moments. "Secrecy is what's kept the peace between our kind for generations."

I pull her against me and kiss her, needing the connection. She returns my kiss, her need mirroring my own.

"When I'm chieftain, I'll consider revealing the dracs to your people." I don't want to be chieftain before my time, but the thought of taking my mate and forging an alliance kindles a hope I don't share out loud.

Dracs don't mix with humans more than necessary—the history of humans and dracs is one of stolen magic and violations against nature. When dracs take human mates, they come to live in the mountains. Even adopted mates honor the secrets that allow us to live in peace. Ophelia's people wouldn't remember what it was like when humans and dracs mixed, when dragons flew over their villages. Though the stories are legend for humans, the dracs remember well.

"My father has been watching your neighboring kingdom, the one skulking on the other side of the mountain."

"Penyasegat?" she says. "Their king is Niklau. He ascended to the throne when his father died suddenly."

"My father is suspicious of his activities. He will never be ready for dracs to reveal themselves. I don't know if we will ever trust humans beyond those that enter our clan as mates."

Ophelia

"I'm just as treacherous as any human," I say playfully, hoping to lighten the serious tone that's settled over us. "And I want you all for myself."

Arik gives me a rueful smile. "Our kinds once lived together, but the humans began hunting us."

"I'm sorry." The words are inadequate. I must recognize my people's part in our shared history. I know the legends, but that's all I thought they were—legend. Until I caught a dragon stalking me in the forest and legend became my reality.

"It was before my time." His gaze drifts to the stars, and I let his serious mood sweep me up in his memories of times before me, before us.

"Over a century ago," I say. These are the stories that children hear in the lowlands when we turn our faces to the mist-covered mountaintops and speculate about the dragon keepers, wondering if there are still dragons. "My people tell stories about it. Dragons only exist as legend, with a few old bones and skulls kept in libraries."

"Aye. Almost two centuries, but my father remembers. That's why he's so strict about dracs interacting with humans."

"But dracs visit the towns in human form," I point out.

He nods. "To trade and to keep an eye on humans. Make sure they don't get it in their heads to hunt dragons. But we've taken great pains to keep humans from knowing that dracs are shifters."

"You could destroy us if we hunted you." It's a sobering thought. If there were ever a conflict, humans would lose.

"Burning down a village would be like burning down a food source," Arik says thoughtfully. His hands glide over my body and slide around my back, pulling me close to him, but his gaze remains on the stars.

I scoff. "You don't eat people," I say, resting my chin on his chest and looking up at his square jaw.

"Not anymore. We don't bloodshed."

I don't want to talk about why dragons and humans can't live together. Why we can't be together. Wishing to live on the dragon peaks with Arik won't change my destiny, and there's no use dwelling on it.

"How do you find your mates?" I change the subject to something lighter.

The question pulls his attention back to us and now. He smiles and looks at me with a lopsided quirk to his lip.

"We know our mates by scent," he says, running lazy fingers over my ass. "It becomes part of us, like unlocking our other half."

I press myself against him and bury my face in his neck. I understand what he means. His briny scent, like a summer breeze on the ocean mixed with vetiver and wind, lives in my mind at all times.

"Our mates have to leave everything behind to live in the mountains," Arik says as if reading my mind.

"If I were drac, I'd have claimed you as mine already," I tell him, trying to keep my disappointment off my face. "But human life spans are so much shorter than dragons' anyway."

Arik gives a small shake of his head. "When a drac takes a human mate, the human's lifespan becomes linked to her mate's, and vice versa. The mated pair would live out their lives together. But if one dies prematurely, their mate will die at the same time."

He inhales deeply. "What do you feel when you take in my scent?"

I press my face against his neck and breathe in deep. His scent enters me, rises to my head, and tingles over my skin. The sensation settles in my chest and fills me with a grounding peace. "Like my soul has found its home." I breathe the words against his neck.

"That's what it feels like when you find your mate," he says with a wide grin. His fingers trace a line up my back, my body coming alive with his scent and his touch.

There's meaning in his smile, and I hold fast, not wanting to read more into his expression.

"You feel it, don't you?" His question is quiet, more assertion than inquiry.

I do feel it. I'm not a drac, but I feel the pull. It's always been there. All this time, he was explaining about matehood. And I knew it. Deep down, I'd felt the rightness when he was near.

My breath hitches. For nearly two years we've met on the new moon and cloudy nights when his winged approach to the castle was concealed by the darkness of a moonless night. He never told me. My heart clenches with sudden fear. Does he not want to claim me?

His eyes soften when he reads my expression, and he whispers, "If you let me take you away, I would claim you as my own. You would be my drac princess."

I can't leave my people. That's why he's never asked.

He places a gentle kiss on my lips. My heart swells so big, I fear it will pound its way out of my chest. Soft kisses turn urgent as we both accept the reality of our situation. I love this man. This beast. This drac. My body responds to the tightening grip of his hands on my back. We are both destined to lead our peoples, but we have each other for now.

He rolls over onto me, the warm shallow water lapping around us. He kisses me softly as he reaches between my legs to stroke my still-slick folds. I gasp into his mouth. He smiles against mine as he presses himself against my entrance. He teases with slow, shallow penetration. I moan, ready for more of him after his lazy attentions to my body.

The press of his body against mine matches the pressure expanding within my chest. The completeness of him and me, of us, that's enveloped us since that first day in the forest.

"Hold on tight," he orders. I obey, desperate to please as well as to feel him. And finally, he sinks inside, filling me completely. He kisses me languidly and fucks me slowly, the long, deep glides of his cock stroking my inner walls.

"I love you," I whisper into the night.

He buries his face in my hair and pulls me tight against his body. I grip him just as hard, fusing him to me, one body, one heartbeat, one breath. His hips pump faster.

I come apart in his arms, my heart breaking a little as I cum around his cock. As my inner walls pulse against him, he pumps hard into me in quick thrusts, drawing out my orgasm as he reaches his own.

We lay there, holding each other for some time before he rolls onto his back and shifts our position so I lay nestled against him.

"I love you," he whispers into the night.

We swim in the warm waters and soak leisurely, whiling away our time together. After playfully trying to dunk each other, he pulls me against him. I wrap my legs around his hips and he lays me back to float on the water. My arms hover over my head, my hair fanning out in the gentle current, and he holds me aloft by the waist. He looks to the skies, and together we gaze up at the starry tapestry and speculate about a limitless horizon.

"I'm never going to marry," I tell the stars. "No matter what happens, the new moon will always be ours."

2

A Slaughtered Drac

Ophelia

Quint's blade slices the air inches from my face. I meet the blow with a decisive counterattack and hurl a quelling look at him. He smiles at me through his bushy, gray-flecked beard. The chief marshal of Devantdemar's army pushes me to my limits, but he insists I never need rely on anyone if I can help it.

I return his blow with my own, which he meets with a deft counter move. We strike and parry until my arms tire, which is the only reason I lose the bout.

Clapping from the steps in front of the great hall draws our attention to King Meynárd, my father, who approaches us with a wide, proud grin.

"Ophelia, you show excellent command of your sword. Quint, you don't let her win anymore?"

"Oh, I don't have to. She wins enough sparring matches on her own."

"Good, good. You continue to amaze me, Ophelia."

"Thank you, Father."

"Quint, we are traveling to Penyasegat this morning. Please ready our escort?"

"Aye, Your Highness." With a quick wink in my direction, the man who's been more like an uncle than anything else takes his leave.

"What's happened?" I ask. Typically, Father does not make journeys without extensive preparation.

"They have felled a dragon in Penyasegat," my father says, a gleam in his eye. "I've just received word from King Niklau. His soldiers brought it down in the fields. He's invited us to come look."

My stomach seizes. "What?" I ask, but I almost don't hear his response as his voice becomes distant and tinny. It's been two weeks since I last saw Arik. He mentioned he and his father were watching Niklau. Who was the drac they felled?

"Yes. I'm traveling there this morning to see."

I don't hesitate. I need to know if it's Arik. "I want to come with you."

"I thought you might," he says with a smile. "Go prepare. We'll be gone more than a week. We'll leave when you're ready."

It's a two-day journey to reach Penyasegat, crossing through the passage that runs between the mountains to the west. It is in the peaks of those mountains where Arik's kind resides. We make good time. Our caravan includes fourteen riders, including my father and me, plus the carriage loaded with our provisions.

I ride my mare Serendipity, but the carriage is an option if I get tired. I would leave the cumbersome transport behind if I could argue a proper reason for doing so. Desperate to see the slaughtered drac, my stomach roils as I set a rapid pace, urging our company on. We make it through the passage and make camp for the night by the time the sun dips below the horizon beyond Penyasegat's canyonlands.

In the morning, I am first to rise. I take it upon myself to rouse the camp before the morning light crests the mountain peaks.

When we arrive at the castle in the late afternoon, an air of festival greets us. As we pass through the gates, we witness the massive, dismembered dragon draped over a flat wagon.

I stop midstep, forcing our company to halt as I process the scene before me. The dragon carcass being butchered is laid out on the flatbed of a cart. I shudder and exhale the breath I'd been holding for two days and a night. The dragon's scales are gray with a purplish tinge, not black with an iridescent blue sheen. This is not my Arik.

All that's left of the carcass is a body with six thick stumps. It's missing its head, tail, and all four legs. It's enormous, maybe bigger than Arik, and turned on its side. Gawkers stand around as butchers and tradespeople work at a gash sliced along the length of its belly. Saliva fills my mouth, and I suppress the urge to vomit with hard swallows.

A white-haired man wearing a blue robe stands on the wagon instructing a butcher what parts to cut. They are systematically disemboweling the majestic beast.

A shiver runs through my body, and I look to the mountain peaks to the east as though I could reach out to my drac with my thoughts. If I were his mate, I could.

My mind races. Who is this drac to Arik? What does this mean for his kind? Or for mine? Will his chieftain retaliate?

There's a commotion as a procession makes its way between the dwellings. King Niklau, riding a white stallion, leads his retinue from the castle. Although he is accompanied by an entourage bearing his colors, he is not dressed in royal regalia. Rather, his dress is casual, more suitable for a ride or for working. He's stocky, a head shorter than my tall and graceful father. Niklau presents himself as a man of the people.

"Greetings, neighbors," he says with enthusiasm as he dismounts and approaches my father. "Welcome, Your Highness." He turns to me. "And to you, Princess Ophelia, welcome."

I curtsy, and my father returns the greeting with equal enthusiasm. "We are honored to receive your invitation," he says. "We would not miss the opportunity to see this great beast."

I paste a smile to my face but turn away when two stable hands approach to take the reins of our mounts.

The dragon is being skinned for its hide. Butchers are cutting away slabs of meat to cook in stew and strips to be smoked and preserved. Mages are extracting bits cut from the organs and placing them in jars.

"It's a pity you couldn't see it intact. He was quite the sight. But he was beginning to smell, and we wanted to salvage as much as possible. This is an immense undertaking."

"Where's the head?" I ask, unable to turn my gaze away from the operations taking place on the wagon.

A member of the king's entourage answers. She's dressed in vibrant blue robes emblazoned with the symbol of a staff engulfed in flames. "It is mounted in the great hall. We've preserved it with magic until we can properly preserve him."

My father studies the woman and then scans the others wearing blue robes. "Mages?"

"Indeed." King Niklau appraises my riding clothes appreciatively, his gaze lingering over my body from my traveling breeches to my tunic and comfortable riding corset. Finally, he assesses my hair, which is bound in a scarf to keep my wild mane from whipping in my face when I ride. Ideally, I would change into attire befitting the meeting of two monarchs, but circumstances do not allow. The flash of approval in his eyes tells me he doesn't mind the breach in protocol.

Niklau is at least ten years older than me. When I was a child, he was preparing to take his place on the throne. On our occasional visits, he took time to spar with me for fun and, as he liked to joke, to gain the measure of the future queen of Devantdemar.

I clutch my hands at my belly to keep from grabbing the sword at my side.

"It's been too long, Princess. Do you still train with your chief marshal?"

"I do, Your Highness."

"Perhaps we will have the opportunity to test your training during your visit, Princess."

His eyes roam my body, and I squeeze my hands to keep from visibly shuddering.

"I'd like that, Your Highness." It isn't a lie. I love a good fight. I wonder if he'd feel the same pain as this drac to be slit from chin to groin.

"You have grown from the bright sprite of a girl I remember into quite the radiant young woman, Princess. I look forward to seeing how you wield a sword."

"Thank you, Your Highness." I turn back to watch the people working on the dragon, unwilling to acknowledge the double entendre.

My father looks on, engrossed as the mage and the butcher gut the dragon with rapt fascination, oblivious to our conversation. The butcher is almost completely submerged in the cavity of the dragon, but he dislodges himself long enough to hand the white-haired mage an organ.

My father asks, "What are the mages doing?"

"My mages are removing the remaining bits for use in spell craft. They've already harvested its magic and removed its major organs and choicest parts."

"How is it you harvest the magic? We have no records that explain the process," my father says, awestruck. "I never believed I'd see it. You are able to harvest it? The legends speak of the dragons' bestowing power."

"I wouldn't call this bestowing magic," I interject.

The two statesmen ignore my comment. "We had the books and parchments, and we knew it was possible. We only lacked the dragons. Recently, there have been sightings. They've been entering our fields and feeding on livestock."

"How did you catch them?" my father asks, moving closer to the carcass, his curiosity overriding his typically reserved manner.

"Using a wee bit of magic, we're able to harvest a great deal more," Niklau says. "We harvest it from the dragons, then use it to catch them."

"Where does one find a 'wee bit of magic'?" my father asks, his focus on the butchering.

I listen as I try to take in everything I see. Arik is not much smaller than the gray dragon sprawled out before us.

"There's magic in every living thing," Niklau explains. "Healers use magic to heal, some without even realizing it. I tasked my librarians to mine the old texts for ways to cultivate their magic. The secret was in the books."

"You said 'them'?" I ask, the knot in my stomach gnarling into a dense mass.

"This is our third dragon. We caught smaller ones recently. We harvested enough magic to prepare for more captures."

"How do you harvest the magic?" I ask, needing to understand more. Does Arik know about this? I have to tell him when I next see him.

"It must be done while the dragon is still alive. Its magic is tied to his life-force."

My vision swims in front of me. I inhale deeply, trying to clear my head, but the air is tinged with the scent of butchered meat that's beginning to turn.

"Amazing," my father says. "And none too soon as it appears that dragons are returning to the canyonlands."

"How did you catch them?" I asked.

"The first dragon was luck. We'd thought dragons were long dead, but a soldier brought one down in the fields. A young one."

My insides clenched again. A drac child?

Bile rises in my throat. My fear for Arik transforms into something else. Dread. This is why the dragons disappeared all those generations ago.

"We are having a feast this night to celebrate our good fortune," King Niklau continues with a note of pride.

Niklau approaches the cart and asks the men working there, "When will you begin removing the hide?"

A prickle runs along the back of my neck, and I scan the throng of people around us. In the crowd I catch the profile of a tall man in a black cloak as he turns to walk away through the crowd. Arik.

I step to follow, but before I can, my father catches my arm and whispers, "Find out what you can about the mages from Niklau. Magic was thought to be long dead. I want to know where these mages come from. He's more likely to share with you than me."

I scan the crowd once more hoping to see Arik. But the cloaked figure is gone. I turn to my father, keeping the body of the fallen drac at my back, no longer able to stomach the slaughtering. "Of course, Father."

In the great hall, the dragon's head is mounted over the hearth. It doesn't have the alarming visage of an attacking animal. Although the drac's eyes are open, the muscles of his face are at rest as though sleeping. Like Arik, he has a wide muzzle and a regal crest protruding from the top of his head like a fan. He looks remarkably like Arik, except for his coloring.

Servers bring us dragon meat. I cannot eat it.

The hair on the back of my neck prickles, and I glance around the great hall looking for Arik.

"I have a gift for you," Niklau says, interrupting my thoughts.

He gestures to his men, and two robed mages approach carrying a tray on which rests a scaly gray and purple claw with long, black nails. I touch the scales with reverence. They feel harder than Arik's. And cooler.

"This is a most gracious gift. We will treasure it always," my father says, giving my arm a squeeze when I don't answer, prompting me to speak through my forced smile.

I turn my gaze to Niklau. "Your mages must be very brave to bring down such an impressive beast. How did they do it?"

I want to know about the mages. I want to know how they're harvesting magic from dragons and how they could kill these majestic beings. And I want to tell Arik everything I learn here so it never happens again.

Arik

My father's head is mounted in the great hall. His eyes have been removed—harvested, as the mages call it—for their magic. The glass eyes inserted in the sockets look out over the proceedings, blind to the revelry at his demise.

Seated to the left of King Niklau, Ophelia hangs on his every word. She reaches to touch the gray scales of my father's claw with a covetous finger. She looks at her father and then turns to look at Niklau with a wide smile. I force myself to watch as my treacherous love accepts the mutilated flesh of my father as a gift while men and women around her laugh, imbibe, and celebrate.

I keep to the shadows. It's been four days since Niklau's men murdered my father, chieftain of the dracs, in a deliberate campaign to trap a dragon with trickery and magic.

Rage fills me and burns in my chest. My initial instinct is to rain fire and raze the castle with the king and all its monstrous inhabitants still inside. My second, Mercé, reminds me that as the new chieftain my responsibility is to keep my people safe, as my father did for over two centuries. A level head is the only way to navigate these uncharted waters, she advises.

My father taught me to be measured, but now his head hangs on the wall. His decapitated, dismembered, rotting corpse is being gutted for its parts. Even now, butchers and mages work to preserve every part of him.

Weeks ago, we lost a curious youth who'd flown down to investigate the farms and had the misfortune to run into the king's soldiers on routine patrol. Caught unawares, the youth was cut down before he'd had a chance to explore the world. The clan suffers for this loss, but the youth's absence from our lives is overshadowed by the humans' brutal agenda and what it might mean for the future of the dracs.

Dracs are not inherently peaceful beings, but we don't decimate populations either. That is also an act against nature. As is stealing magic and using it to kill. Dracs have always sought to maintain balance. Our very existence is a balance between instinct, reason, and magic. We will not be drawn into a war. Mercé is right. Now is the time to mourn. And plan.

Ophelia

The journey home is pensive and slower, having lost the urgency of our arrival. I am silent for much of our ride, until I can no longer hold my tongue. "This is a great tragedy, Father."

He turns to me. "The discovery of magic?"

"The killing of those dracs...dragons."

I look to the mountain peaks, shrouded in their mist. My father replies, "Aye. But look at the gains. And the return of dragons. And their magic."

"Father, those noble people—creatures—they don't deserve to be cut down like that." I force calm to my voice, though my heart is racing, desperate to see Arik. To hold him. To tell him what I've seen and heard.

"Daughter, if Niklau has magic, the only way we can maintain an equal footing with our neighboring kingdoms and preserve the peace we enjoy is to have magic also. The mountain pass is our most direct link to the interior lands without having to travel for weeks along the coast."

Does my father mean to obtain magic for Devantdemar? The thought curdles my breakfast in my stomach.

We maintain an ambling pace under the shadow of the mountain. My father's gaze glances over mountains and canyons, but never settles on mine.

"Our relationship with Niklau is friendly, but the minute he has any kind of advantage over us, we become weak in his eyes. Trading seafood and grains and providing access to the sea holds no power against the potential of magic."

"The dragon keepers are our neighbors as well, and their dealings with us are peaceful."

"If they let loose their dragons to feed on neighboring livestock, it should be expected that farmers will take one or two down."

"What if the dragons exact revenge? On what side of that battle do you want to be on?" I prod.

My father scoffs. "Dragons take revenge?"

"I mean the dragon keepers."

"Dragons are mindless beasts. Although the dragon keepers come down from the mountain to trade, there has been no sighting of a dragon since before my father's time."

"This isn't the first dragon they felled, Father. And the dragons know. They know the way you would know if I went missing."

I turn my face to the mountain peaks before we round the bend leading through the mountain passage to our coastal lands. On the next new moon, I'll talk to my drac and tell him everything I've learned.

3

A Betrothal

Ophelia

Two years have passed since I saw my dragon. I waited for him on the night of the Spring Feast. Then I waited for him on the new moon. And on every cloudy night and new moon after that. He never comes.

Six dragons have been felled in Penyasegat. Two small dragons were captured two years ago, before the large one that we saw butchered that day we traveled to the kingdom through the mountain pass. Now there is word that three more smaller ones have been felled.

There are no dragon sightings on Devantdemar's ocean side of the mountains. I know that dragons hunt for their food in the ocean in the dead of night. We don't keep the extensive livestock that the Penyasegat do. Perhaps that's the attraction for the dragons there.

We receive invitations to join Niklau to celebrate the downed dragons, and each time my father and I journey to our neighboring lands. On each visit, I travel with my heart in my throat, desperate with fear that the next dismembered body will be Arik's. Each time I come home with a renewed hope that my dragon will return to me.

Is he dead? As painful as it is to recognize, it is a small relief to think he stays away because he no longer wants me, and not because he has perished. With the slaughter of each dragon, hope for his return dies a little more. I'm not a fool. My heart makes its journey from where it's lodged in my throat to where it aches in my chest each time I return home.

For two years, Father has had his clerics scouring our libraries for any information on magic—and, to my consternation, dragons. I haunt them, hoping to learn something about dracs or their magic. Or even steal the books they find. But the librarians have discovered only that texts are missing. Anything about magic or dragons is gone. For my father, visits to Penyasegat are fact-finding expeditions as much as friendly relations.

Over breakfast a few days after the winter solstice, my father tells me, "We've just received word from Penyasegat."

My heart sinks. Another drac?

"King Niklau will arrive three days hence."

"Visiting here?" I'm flushed with the disorienting wave of relief and confusion.

"Yes. He will arrive with his army."

"Army? Is he waging war?" I ask, unable to keep the surprise from my voice.

"According to his message," he says with eyebrows raised, "he has a proposition for me."

A knot forms in my belly. What could he possibly be proposing? Are my father's concerns over a political imbalance being borne out? Foreboding, my constant companion, settles deeper in my stomach.

Over the next few days, we launch into a frenzy of activity, preparing the castle and the surrounding lands. Quint is tasked with readying our fighting forces and ensuring our village militias are prepared. I stay busy working with the castle servants to prepare for King Niklau and his entourage's visit. Our scholars are tasked with preparing to host Niklau's mages.

I hope Niklau's proposal has to do with agricultural trade and not with magic. Or, more unsettling, me.

When Niklau arrives, my father, normally a charismatic and self-assured monarch, is nervous. The rumors of increased dragon sightings on the canyon side of the mountain overlooking Penyasegat and the occasional loss of livestock, paired with Niklau's mages' increasing mastery of magic, make my father anxious. To what lengths will he go to gain magic? Especially now that Niklau brings his army into our lands.

There has been no drac retaliation. Arik's father always advised peace and isolation. Is this still the case? Or are they planning something?

"Dragons are not raiding our farms," I tell the two kings from my seat on the windowsill in the study overlooking the courtyard.

Niklau sits in the study with three mages in flowing blue robes at his back.

"It's because the Devantdemar side of the mountain is more easily accessible. We believe that they are not provoking you because it's too easy for you to reach them to retaliate. Whereas we cannot access the keepers from the Penyasegat side," Niklau responds, "since the passes on our side are inaccessible. I want to travel to the dragon peaks on this side of the mountain."

He leans forward, resting his forearms on his thighs. "I want to negotiate trade with the dragon keepers."

"Negotiate?" my father asks, repeating Niklau.

"With an army?" I ask, less diplomatically, and my father shoots me a look.

"Yes. It's time we met these mysterious dragon keepers, since their dragons have been acquainting themselves with our farms."

"That's not possible," I interject from my perch. "The dragon keepers are a peaceful clan. They raise mountain goats to feed their dragons."

"That we know of." Niklau has his answers at the ready. "Perhaps they've lost their herds. Otherwise, why raid our farms?"

"We've had no such trouble."

"Perhaps they've come upon hard times. Perhaps the dragons have overrun the keepers."

"You'd bring an army to negotiate?" I ask again.

"There are too many questions, Princess. One that's been on my mind for some time is, how long will the dragons be satisfied with sheep and cattle?"

The claim is spurious, a false justification for his magic mongering. More livestock is lost to wolves or illness than to dragons. Why can't my father see that?

"If we allow them to continue, we run the risk of our kingdoms being overrun by dragons. We need to address the problem in their lands. We need to demonstrate that we can not only defend ourselves, but that we can..." He pauses briefly when I turn my gaze to meet his before continuing, "...retaliate."

Retaliate?Against dragons? I almost snap back, but I hold my tongue and level an argument drawn from diplomacy instead. "If they wanted to do damage, they would have long ago."

"How would you know anything about dragons?"

I ignore the question. We cannot send armies to the dragon keeper territories under false pretenses. "Father, allow me to go as your emissary to meet with the dragon keepers."

"These dragon keepers are barbarians," Niklau says.

"How do you know if you haven't seen them?" I argue, aware that my diplomatic mask has slipped. "They enter the Devantdemar villages peacefully to trade. We don't even know when they've been here until they've come and gone. They have friends in the villages, and in some cases family. The villagers speak only kindly of the ones they trade with regularly."

My father knows this to be true. He rubs the back of his neck but remains silent.

I cannot argue with the king in front of our visitors, but I want to shake him. The specter of magic cannot hold him in such thrall. Not for the first time, I'm flushed with the need to ride to Arik's village. But his two-year absence has made it clear. He wants nothing to do with me. Maybe he's found a drac mate. I push down that fear. The knowledge would destroy me.

Niklau eyes me curiously. Then he sighs heavily as he lifts his gaze to the window over my shoulder toward the mountain.

"I have a proposition." The fabric of his rich garments rustles as he stands, and he takes a few heavy steps toward us. "I propose an alliance between Devantdemar and Penyasegat."

I listen hard, wrestling the mask of cool, regal detachment back onto my face.

"I would like to formally request a union between the beautiful princess Ophelia and myself to unite our two kingdoms."

My face is stone. I risk no reaction to his words. I'm eight and twenty. Well beyond marriable years for a commoner. But I am not a commoner. I've made it clear to my father I won't marry, and he's always supported my intentions. As queen, I will not need a partner to co-rule, and my younger sisters have already produced a gaggle of heirs. My father has ruled alone with the help of his privy council for decades.

"I—"

"Ophelia and I will discuss your proposal."

Now he chooses to interject? I look at my father, stunned, before sliding my mask of diplomatic comportment back into place. I don't miss the unspoken warning my father directs at me. We will indeed be discussing it.

"Allied, we could join our armies and approach the dragon keepers to investigate and offer aid if needed. But together, we offer each other protection if we encounter trouble. And since I would be gaining a wife, I would happily lend one of our mages to train your people in the art of magic."

With that promise of magic, hope of a balanced discussion is lost for now.

An acquisitive spark flashes in my father's eyes, and I know what he's going to say before he opens his mouth. "I have often thought about forging an alliance between our two kingdoms."

I almost groan, but my diplomatic training overrides the impulse.

Niklau smiles at this. "We can begin exercising our alliance with a joint expedition to the peaks. How long would it take you to get your forces assembled?"

"Our soldiers are always at the ready," my father says, not giving away that we've been rallying our forces for three days already.

"Father—"

"Ophelia, we will discuss the details after dinner." My father's tone brooks no argument. We will discuss our new alliance tonight, but it's clear his decision has been made. "Go get Quint."

Dismissed. Just like that. A stern reminder I am not yet queen.

Turning back to Niklau, my father says, "We should not advance on the keepers as an army."

I linger in the doorway to listen.

"You're right, of course." Niklau agrees quickly. Concessions are easy to make when you've already won the battle. "We will take our armies to the mountains and build camp. Then you and I will proceed with an entourage to meet the dragon keepers."

"That is an acceptable solution. We will announce the betrothal at the Spring Feast."

I bristle at my father's plotting. He is not a calculating man. When did I become a bargaining chip? The treachery of humans and their lust for magic. This is why dracs work so hard to keep humans from acquiring magic beyond what's naturally endowed to us.

"For now," my father tells Niklau, who turns a piercing gaze on me, "we can proceed as a united front to the dragon keep at the peak."

I will not marry Niklau. I will not marry anyone. I will rule Devantdemar as queen one day. But I have time to deal with the marriage problem. First, my father and Niklau intend to advance to the dragon keep with the armed forces of two nations. The spike of betrayal would have pierced my heart if the fire in my chest hadn't already incinerated it.

I need to get word to Arik, even if he never wants to see me again.

Sneaking out of the castle in the middle of the night is easier on the wings of a dragon. On my own, I must creep down the back passage to the kitchens. I carry only the warm layers of clothing on my body, my dagger and long blade, and a skin of water. Retrieving my mare from the stables is easy due to the disruption of boarding horses for Niklau and his retinue. Leaving through the gates is also easy with the commotion of the visiting legion and the preparation of our own troops.

Dressed in leather riding breeches and hooded under a heavy black cloak, I am indistinguishable from the soldiers in the camp outside our gates. I canter with casual purpose at the perimeter of the camp, until I am well enough beyond the field of tents and war machines. Once I pass the last of the tents, we break into a run and ride hard for the foothills.

I must warn Arik. Niklau's intentions are not to negotiate trade deals. That's apparent to anyone who doesn't share his ambitions. He wants to harvest more magic, and he is going straight to the source. Perhaps warning Arik will allow us to find a solution and prevent bloodshed.

I also want to see him. I want to see in his eyes that he no longer thinks of me.

4

A Drac on His Peak

Arik

Winds course through the rocky mountaintop landscape, whipping between the corridors of natural formations. Young dragons jump into the wind, catching the current, flinging themselves into the sky, and disappearing into the mist. Mountain goats graze at the tufts of hard grass that speckle the landscape. The cloud bank obscures our view of the coastline below.

I stand at the entrance of the grand cavern in my human form, enjoying the early morning calm as I witness the growing bustle of dracs emerging from smaller cave entrances to start the day.

Dragon magic is the force that allows dragons to shift. It allows us to heal. It allows us to cloak ourselves for brief moments. There is magic in every living thing. Long ago, humans learned how to access their own magic in its limited power. They cultivated the ability to enhance the power of the natural elements such as toxins from plants or rain from vapor. Those talented with magic and proficient in its manipulation were called mages. They use toxins against each other in war. At some point, they discovered how to access the magic in dragons with minor spellcraft. And they learned how to use the magic harvested from dracs to take down our drac to harvest more magic. We believed we had seized and secured all magic texts in the libraries of the kingdoms surrounding our peaks. Yet a mage in Niklau's kingdom found the way to access dragon magic. I never disagreed with my father's decrees, but the sense of futility that weighs on me wars with my need to bridle the insidious nature of humankind.

Dracs keep to the mountains for a reason, aside from enjoying the gales and the rough terrain of the peaks. We have no interest in war. And the mixing of our kind with others, especially the avaricious humans, has always led to war.

I saw a different side to humans when I met Ophelia, my mate. The pull to claim her as mine was overwhelming, but I resisted it. Then, as I got to know her, I understood that magic drives the mating bonds. It was magic that made it possible for her to spy me in the forest—a feat that would have been impossible otherwise. She was perfect for me. Her adventurous heart, her political savvy, and her compassionate intellect ensnared me as much as her scent and smile. I welcomed the seductive well of matehood longing, despite our conflicting responsibilities. I entertained the fantasy of claiming her and revealing the dual natures of the dracs once again. I just wanted her.

But King Niklau's ambitions and his sadistic realization of those ambitions has demonstrated once again why dracs and humans cannot mix. If I am to prioritize the well-being of my kind, as my father did before me, I have to choke off the bone-deep yearning.

Mercé's footsteps approach behind me. Her words are clipped. "Angus has returned with news."

"Tell me."

"Niklau has gifted the head of one of the youths, Lander, to the Devantdemar king," my second says.

A groan of disgust escapes my lips.

"Arik, they were told to stay out of those fields. It's not your fault."

My oldest friend, and now chief advisor, has been trying to assuage my guilt since we received word that the three adventurous youths ventured into the Penyasegat farmlands to nab a sheep. Despite my mandate to stay out of human lands, it's become sport for our most daring youths to test their skills. They coast low to steal livestock, and though they remain unseen, the mages have laid traps that ensnare large airborne predators. The daring and rebelliousness are understandable—expected for drac youths testing their boundaries. The young dracs believe themselves invincible, but the mages have learned new tricks and become stronger since they harnessed my father's magic. Now more youths are lost to us forever.

The clan is torn between retaliating and maintaining our reclusive existence. Retaliation would mean revealing ourselves, and as my father and my grandfather before him argued, exposure would rekindle the old threats.

Yet is a life of isolation fair? With Ophelia, I envisioned revealing ourselves and integrating with humankind in time.

"It is still my responsibility to keep them safe," I say. The same argument I've used each time we lose another clanmate. Six in little more than two years.

"The Devantdemar people have not acquired a taste for drac blood."

"It's only a matter of time. From what Vanka and our other spies tell us, King Meynárd is drawn to the magic as well. He is searching."

"We have been trading as keepers with Devantdemar for ages. They have never given any indication of wanting dragons, aside from a natural curiosity," she says.

"King Niklau has been gifting them pieces of our friends for two years. It's only a matter of time before they seek to capture their own dragons."

"There's more, Arik. Niklau has arrived at Devantdemar with a throng of armed soldiers."

My attention snaps to her, surprised by the news. "To attack?"

"To form a union. Niklau has proposed marriage to the oldest princess. Ophelia."

The image of Ophelia tracing her fingers over the lusterless gray scales of my father's dismembered claw flashes in my mind. The quiet contemplation that crossed her face when she did. She loved running her hands over my scales. What had been going through her mind when she stroked the scales of the claw? I'll never know. Regardless, humans can't be trusted.

I should've killed her when I realized my mate was human. She's one of the few humans that know dragon keepers and dracs are shifter beings, and the only such human not adopted into our clan. Would she tell her father? Her new husband? It was only a matter of time.

I often descend to the palace on moonless nights, intent on incinerating her with a blast of dragon fire to ensure she never reveals our secrets. Instead, I watch her on the garden terrace as she looks to the skies. Watching for me. I can't destroy her any more than I could tear off my own wings. Yet each time I let her live, I feel like I am betraying my people. My father.

She is my weakness. My heart pounds in my chest thinking about her. Or rather, her treachery. She said she'd never marry.

"Is that all?" I ask, eager to end the brief.

"One more thing. Our scouts captured a spy trying to reach our peaks."

"Where are they? Have you spoken with them?"

"Not yet. They took her directly to the lower caverns. She's asked to speak with you. What would you like to do with her?"

"I should speak to her. Leave her in the dungeons to soften a bit. I'll go down later. I'd like to know what Niklau intends with his army."

"We also have her horse."

I turn to face her at that, eyebrow raised. "She rode a horse up the mountain?"

"As far as the tree line," Mercé answers with a note of admiration. It takes a fair bit of horsemanship to ride to the tree line that marks the mountainside forest and the rocky peaks where only brush grows. "Then she left it to climb on foot. That's where our scout captured her."

"The horse is here?"

"Yes." Mercé points toward the pens, which are built into a smaller cave nestled at the base of the ravine beneath the great cavern entrance where we keep mountain goats and other livestock.

I lean forward to peer over the ledge where I stand. My mouth goes dry when I see the chestnut mare, nervous and excitable, being walked along the ravine below. Serendipity. "That's the princess's horse."

Mercé pales. "She's dressed in riding clothes. Our scouts didn't recognize her. Do you want me to bring her up?"

"No. I'll deal with her." I turn on my heel and enter the cave, intent on questioning the princess spy.

5

A Captured Princess

Arik

In the upper levels of the caverns, tunnels from the surface cast light on the common areas. I stride down the carved path below. Torches and candles light the more trafficked passages for the humans of our clan, and phosphorescent walls illuminate the great halls, the tunnels that branch off, and the residences. In other areas, the darkness is absolute.

In the depths, where we store food and supplies and keep the occasional prisoner, there is no light, natural or unnatural. Dracs can see perfectly in the dark. I stride down elaborately carved steps to the lower caverns.

My heart pounds heavy in my chest, but I keep the image of her look of wonder as she held my father's claw in her hands at the forefront of my thoughts.

She's betrothed to Niklau, I remind myself.

I bring forth the memory of the youths and their rebellious antics and the knowledge they will never return to their families. They will never again race the winds through the ravines with their cohort.

The last time I was with Ophelia, her body glistening on the waters of the hot springs, she said she'd keep my secrets. Has she? My spies would have caught word if the lowlanders discovered that dragon keepers were in fact the dragons they were thought to keep.

I approach the cold chamber where she's being held, my footfalls silent. There are no doors on the cells. It's too dark for humans to see, and the manacles are sufficient to keep prisoners in place.

I cross the threshold, and I'm immersed in her scent like dropping into a cloud bank. Berries and honeyed musk. My mate. My dick grows hard, every cell in my body compelling me to claim her. The need only stokes my anger. I should want to hurt her, but the need to claim her as my mate prickles over my entire being.

Quietly I approach, watching her. She sits in the dark on the ground, huddled and leaning against the rock wall. Her hands are bound with iron manacles, connected by a chain threaded through a loop at the base of the wall. There's no need for guards since a human can't hope to escape chains that could hold a drac, and the silence in isolation is absolute. Her eyes are closed, and she's shaking with cold.

When my boot crunches sand, she looks up with a start. Her eyes widen, struggling to take in what stray light they can find. But she's blind. She licks her lips nervously, turning her head searching like she's listening hard.

I study her treacherous, heart-shaped face.

How I was fooled by her. Taken in by her beauty when I met her that day climbing over boulders in the foothills. She was bold and indomitable, and I'd been lost to her infectious laughter. And then later, when I approached, to her scent.

Dracs find their mates through scent. Although I hadn't known it then, hers had entered me, placed a hold on me, and drawn me back to her over and over. Now the impulse to protect her wars with my need for vengeance. For justice.

I watch. Her eyes are dark pools, her pupils enlarged, desperate to catch any small bit of light.

I gird myself before saying, "What do we have here?"

In a move erotic in its deftness, she shifts to stand on her knees. She swings one arm overhead to scuttle toward me. Her arms pull back taut on either side, straining against the chains and holding her back as she lunges forward. Her smile is radiant and fearless.

"Arik," she whispers in the dark. "I knew you'd come."

Ophelia beams at me from her kneeling position, her arms pulled behind her, exposing her throat and underbelly. I'd forgotten she radiates her own light.

When I don't respond, she says, "It's me. Ophelia." Her eyes are wide and seeking. As if I wouldn't know her.

I cup her jaw firmly, not wanting to hear the sweetness in her voice. I can't afford to believe anything out of her beautiful mouth. But she presses her cheek into my hand and inhales.

"It's you, isn't it?"

I kneel in front of her. "Ophelia." Her name comes out as a croak.

She tries to scuttle closer, but her arms are again pulled back by the chains. She raises her face to mine, seeking my heat like a sunflower turning to the sun. Her scent fills my head, clouding my reason.

It's been two years since that night at the hot springs, when she wrapped her body around mine, clinging to me, promising to never marry. To be mine and mine alone on moonless nights.

Kindling memories, a heat enters my chest, warming a place that had been colder than these rock walls. I call it rage and conjure images of my father's disemboweled body on display.

I shake my head to clear the fog. What is she planning with Niklau? Why are they attacking now?

The words are on the tip of my tongue, but instead my mouth comes down hard on hers. I intend to punish her, my tongue firmly penetrating her mouth, but she opens to me, meeting my tongue and punishing me in return.

Lost to her, I extend a sharp claw, slice the laces of her riding corset, and tear her tunic open. I swallow her gasp as I slash at the cloth binding her breasts. She tries to press against me, a futile effort again stopped by the pulling chains.

Ophelia

I welcome the biting strain in my shoulders as I lean forward toward my love. His presence sends tingles coursing through my body. His long absence and all the fears I'd brooded over for the past two years are chased away by the low rumble of his voice, replaced by the haunted longing that his proximity incites. My nipples grow tight, but not for the chill in the room. I tremble, but I'm no longer cold.

He lifts me to my feet. I can barely stand upright with my arms chained to the ground. He works the boots roughly off my feet and slashes at the belt of my riding breeches. They drop to the floor.

His warm face presses to my mound, and he inhales deeply. A hand slides up the inside of my leg, and I step wide, eager for his touch. I'm his. Even after two years, that hasn't changed.

His fingers spread my folds, and his tongue slips into my slit to lick my clit as he slides two fingers inside me. I'm slick from the sound of his voice, from his still-familiar scent, and from his tongue claiming me after so long. His big fingers slide in easily, filling me.

"Arik," I whisper. I reach to grip his hair with both hands, but the chains stop me with a loud rattle.

"Shut up," he whispers as he pulls me down to straddle his lap.

Closer to the ground there's more give in the chains, but I still can't touch him. Fabric shifts against fabric, then his thick cock is pressing against my entrance.

"Arik," I say, alarmed. I'm wet, but he's huge.

Then he jerks me down onto him, impaling me with an angry thrust and a guttural moan. I cry out as my body tries to reconcile the sting of my flesh with the delicious heat of his hard cock.

Desperate to hold him, my fingers flex in the iron cuffs. He grips me tight, one hand on my hip, the other pressed against my back, pinning me down on him. I drop my head back and breathe deep.

There were many days when I'd walked with the delicious soreness from his harsh and desperate fucking, but this was different. Where once he was gentle, easing himself into me and eventually leaving me swollen and sore, now he seems driven by a need that eclipses any tenderness. But I welcome the sting—anything he'll give me—grateful to be in his arms again.

He stills, his cock seated fully inside me, the tension in his body radiating into mine through our skin. My body shudders against him as I relax on his cock. I know what comes next, and every part of me is ready for him. It's all I've wanted for so long.

"Arik. My—"

His mouth crashes onto mine, his tongue penetrating me as he pulls back and then thrusts his hips to fill me again.

With his arm wrapped around my back, he leans me against the wall. He pulls out slowly, stroking my inner walls. Then he thrusts back into me roughly, and the contrasting sensation of sweet satisfaction and grasping sting clash within me. Soft and hard. Want and fear. Regret and need.

"Arik," I whisper against his mouth, urging him on. "I've dreamed of this for so long."

He laughs. "Dreamed of me fucking you on the floor of a cave, Princess?" The edge in his voice is sharp and exciting.

I don't answer. I can't see his face, but his tone is mocking.

He shifts our position, pulling us forward, and lays me on the hard ground. Impaled on his cock, I can do nothing. Like this, there's enough slack in the chain that I can reach his shoulders and chest now. I run my hands over his hard muscles, slick with sweat. He thrusts into me again. And again.

The grit on the floor cuts into my back. He squeezes my hip mercilessly. There's no gentleness. The sheer need radiating off him fuels my own. I don't fear him. I only want him, my body responding to his lurid hunger. *Fuck me. Use me. Love me.*

My core tightens. I'm so close. He bucks into me wildly.

"Please," I beg.

Then with no warning, he pulls out. I hear him grunt and then the wet smack of what can only be him stroking himself urgently. I feel him shudder, and then the hot spurts of his cum on my belly and breasts.

"Arik?" I ask, confused.

Again he says nothing, letting out a low groan as he massages his cum slowly into my skin. I'm gripped with an overwhelming sense of desolation. First in my body and then in my soul. His withdrawal feels absolute.

The chains clank before I feel his hands at my wrist, releasing one iron cuff, then the other. He says nothing when he cradles me in his arms and lifts me. Though the tension in his body keeps me from settling in against him, the way he pulls me against him is tender. He's chaos under his rigid exterior.

"Arik, I need to talk to you."

"Later," he says as we move through the dark. I'm unable to see as he navigates the dark easily. Of course. Dracs can see in the dark. He was watching me. Has he been watching me all this time?

We emerge from a dark tunnel into a chamber lit by low green light emanating from the walls. He is unconcerned by my nakedness as we pass two men at the entrance of another dark tunnel. We move through chamber after chamber connected by dark tunnels, passing drac along the way. I refuse to cower in shame. I hold my head upright and survey the caverns, meeting the gaze of anyone who looks upon me in the dimly lit tunnels.

A door opens.

Arik addresses a man and a woman standing guard. Although he speaks in drac, I recognize a few words. "Alert me... foothills." Neither looks at me as we walk in.

The ornate door closes behind us. We pass through a luxuriously appointed seating area before an enormous fireplace carved into the rock wall. In the firelight, I see the walls are artfully sculpted into flowing patterns of swirling and rippling water.

We enter another chamber. Wall sconces with candles cast a soft flickering light throughout the room. An enormous canopied bed stands against the far wall, and I can't help but wonder if he sleeps here in his dragon form. Does he sleep alone?

He kicks the door closed behind us, and then he drops me unceremoniously onto the bed.

"Arik," I say again, looking at his face for the first time. My heart stops beating in my chest. He's beautiful. And angry.

Arik

I'm ensorcelled by her scent, the same berry and honeyed musk infused in my soul during our many moonless nights together. The drive to claim her pounding in my head, my chest, my gut, and in my skin. But I resist.

I force myself to remember that she's human. No different from the rodents scurrying on the valley floor, until they get their hands on magic and unleash horrors on each other and the natural world. It's why we retreated to the mountains all those generations ago. Over the years, our drac spies have appropriated the books that held human insights to magic. But the human mages secreted away some texts, and once again they are committing crimes against nature, against my kind, in their self-serving pursuit of magic and power.

"Arik, I need to talk to you."

"Later." Right now, I need to fuck her out of my system.

I push her onto her back, spread her legs, and press my face into her cunt, desperate to get to the source of her scent. To saturate myself with it. To sate myself so I can purge her from my system. I run my tongue from her asshole to her clit, tasting her intoxicating juices.

I can have this, just a taste, and then she can go back to her treacherous magic-grubbing people.

Claim her, a force from the marrow of my bones demands of me.

I could—should—mark her as mine with my seed, my scent, and my bite to consummate our bond. I could be complete for once and for all, instead of living this half existence, knowing my mate is out there. I could keep her here.

She spreads her legs wide, silent, inviting, wanting. The words are on the tip of my tongue—*good princess*—but she doesn't deserve my praise.

I raise my gaze to look at her face. She is on her elbows watching me, panting, eyes wide. I drive two fingers inside her and pump hard as I circle her clit with my tongue. She bucks, trying to grind against me. I increase my pace, fucking her with my fingers.

I can resist. I can watch her come apart this one last time and send her back to her people to wage this senseless war. If I send her back to her palace, she'll be safe. If I send her back to the army, she'll perish in the blaze that is her army's fate.

Her body tightens, and I know she's on the edge. I could deny her again, but I want her to cum all over me. I want to bathe in her scent.

I nip at her clit as I add another finger, pumping her cunt furiously.

"Cum," I command.

Her cunt grips my fingers, and her body goes limp, head and shoulders slumping against the bed. Her moans of pleasure accompany the wet smacking of my thrusting fingers and lapping tongue. Her inner walls pulse around my fingers, and her orgasm drips through my hands.

I never loved so hard as I love her. My heart cramps, knowing I cannot have her. That my princess can never be mine. The need to bond with my mate wars with my loathing of humans. I force down the torrent of internal turmoil and focus on her face and the play of sensations I see there.

I grip my cock in my hand and stroke myself.

"This is what you came for, isn't it? Dragon cock?"

"No, Arik—" She sobers at my words. I pump my fingers faster, distracting her from thought, preventing her from coming out of her lust-filled haze. She moans in response.

Her pussy is still pulsing around my fingers when I flip her onto her hands and knees.

Ophelia

There is nothing else. Just Arik and me and this, one body. I came here for him. I don't deny it. "Yes," I admit when he lifts my hips. "Arik—" My words falter as he sinks his cock into my slick heat again.

He drives inside me once and holds himself still, groaning as my pussy pulses around him in my lingering orgasm. He spreads my ass cheeks open. His thumb, slick with my own juices, presses against my ass. Then he's pushing the digit inside me, filling me completely. The slight burn gives way to depraved bliss.

I grip the sheets over my head and push back against him, urging him on.

"Arik," I moan his name.

"Yes, my filthy princess?"

"Please," I beg. "Fuck me." With his thumb and his cock inside me, the fullness presses against me from within.

Then he drags his cock out slowly, hissing as he pulls out. My nerves buzz at the tight, decadent friction. I moan loudly against the soft sheets until he stops. I arch my back, ready to take him. He doesn't make me wait. He slams into me, pounding fast and hard. His fingers bite into my fleshy hips as his cock strokes my inner walls feverishly.

Primed from my last orgasm, yet barely recovered, I topple into another wave of ecstasy.

Arik

My balls tighten as I watch my cock disappear inside her grasping cunt. I moan at the unexpected sensation, and then I'm cumming hard in her. After pumping into her, shuddering my final thrusts, I resist the urge to fall on her and pull her to me. Instead, I slide out of her and stand next to the bed.

She rolls onto her back. She's sated and flushed, arms and legs seductively splayed, eyes closed, cunt dripping with our combined cum. One good thing comes of not claiming my mate—babies can't happen without the bond, so there's no risk of sending her home with a drackling to be exploited.

A knock sounds at the door, and I pull myself away from the bed.

Outside my chambers, Mercé stands holding a bundle. "They've been mended."

I take the clothes she offers and note my second's concerned expression. Mercé is the only one who knows that I found my mate years ago. Back then, she championed me claiming the princess as my mate. Now she's lying in my bed, her people responsible for killing our chieftain, my father. The pity in Mercé's eyes flays me.

"Take her back to her people when she's ready," I say, my voice tight.

"Aye, Arik." Her voice is soft, compassionate, but I don't miss the ease that settles in her shoulders. Although others of our kind have taken human mates, my people would never accept a human wife for the chieftain when her people—the people she is to one day lead—stand on our mountain poised to attack us.

"It's for the best, Arik."

"It is," I say.

Ophelia

Arik strides back from the door and stands over me.

"I came to talk to you," I say, sated and sobering from my sex-muddled state. "I came to tell you—"

"Your betrothed is on his way up your side of the mountain with a contingent of armed men."

I sit upright. "That's what I came to tell you. My father sent men too."

"I thought you just came for my cock."

I ignore the jibe. "Niklau has recruited my father. I wanted to warn you." While I was reveling in his scent, his heat, his touch, he was stabbing me with his body, his heart, and his hate. Only now do I feel the cuts.

How can one that allows her body to deceive her so be trusted to lead a people?

"It looks more like you were trying to distract me." There's an edge to his voice that drags me back from my self-loathing. "So your father and your betrothed have allied."

"No," I say, but I falter. "Yes. I mean, they have, but he's not my betrothed."

He grabs my jaw with a firm grip and says, "I don't believe anything out of your mouth. Especially now that both your armies are united and advancing."

"Please, listen—"

"You came here for cock or to spy." His words are clipped. "Which is it?"

I rise to my knees, wanting to crawl to him, to curl into his lap, and talk to him the way we used to after making love. But I hold his gaze and say, "I demand to be heard."

He releases me and rises to his full height. Maybe he means to intimidate me, but he's never hurt me before. Not in a way I didn't welcome, anyway.

"You have said nothing I don't already know," he says.

I can't hide my shock from the perceptive black eyes bearing into me.

"What do you think?" His tone is mocking. "Of course, I know they're here. How do you think our scouts found you? You think I don't have spies in your lands?"

The breath leaves my body. "You've been there?" There's a hole left where I've been punched in the chest. "You've been watching all this time."

"I visit frequently." His look is dismissive.

I believed the death of the dragons caused him to stay away. He hadn't stayed away after all. He just hadn't been there to see me.

"I'm chieftain now—"

"Chieftain?" Clutching the sheets in my fists, I don't hide my surprise. That means his father is dead.

"I will defend my dracs from your kind. As we always have."

I don't hear his words as I'm struck by the memory of Arik cloaked in Penyasegat when the big dragon was felled. I had been so relieved that it wasn't Arik, I hadn't thought who it could be. Of course. Arik is chieftain now.

"Your father," I say behind him. "He was one of the dracs that Niklau felled." It's not a question. The answer is in his haunted eyes and hardened jaw.

"It was my father's claw that Niklau gifted you at the banquet. Don't you remember?" He tosses my clothes onto the bed and without looking at me turns to leave.

Grabbing his breeches from the ground, he stalks out of the room naked, his finely chiseled form lithe and commanding. Over his shoulder, he says, "The guards will take you back."

"Arik," I call out. "I demand to be heard."

I dress quickly to follow him. The garments Arik tore in the dungeons are mended, and I'm careful not to tear the stitching. The tunic is barely over my head when I run out of the room, but a drac stops me. She hands me my dagger and long blade and allows me to strap them on before carefully placing a sack over my head.

"I need to talk to Arik," I insist and move to follow him.

She steps in front of me. "We have orders to return you to your people." Her words are clipped, but her gentle manner belies the admonishment in her tone.

Another drac lifts me in his arms, and within moments, we emerge into crisp air, sunlight leaking into the sack over my head. Then without warning, we're airborne.

Two talons loop under each of my arms, gripping my shoulders, and I'm dangling in the cold mountain winds. I see nothing above or below. I grab the claws for dear life as I kick wildly at nothing. I'm going to vomit. I'd flown with my drac lover at night before, safe on his back or cradled in his foreclaws. Flying like this, blindfolded and dangling, I am not safe. My body goes rigid, the fear of being dropped freezing my muscles.

"Here's where we drop you," a growly, masculine voice says.

I brace myself for a long fall, but when the dragon lets go, the drop is only a few feet. I'm not ready for it, and the ground comes at me hard. A sharp pain explodes in my ankle, and I cry out.

I hear one quick snap of wings, then silence.

6

An Accusation

Ophelia

The steep downward slope beneath my feet and the position of the sun above my head are the only indications of where I am. The armies must be close for the drac to have dropped me here. We're nearer to the peak than the foothills. I remove the sack from my head to look out and take in the view of my homeland nestled between mountain and sea, with its rich farmlands and miles of sandy beaches. Arik's view of my kingdom is breathtaking.

I take tentative steps through the sparse underbrush, sharp pain streaking from my ankle up through my leg. Barely able to walk, I find a branch to support my weight. I'm able to limp a few steps before exhaling and blowing hair out of my face.

The sun has not reached its zenith and there is still mist on the ground. It must be midmorning, but I have no sense of how long I've been gone. Maybe a day and a night, but the countless hours in the dark could have been a week.

Foolish girl. I'd convinced myself of a half dozen scenarios since he last visited me, but I never wanted to believe that he just didn't want to see me. The knowing is a clamp around my heart, the pain a thousand times worse than the wondering. I feel nothing else.

Voices sound through the enormous pines as I limp downhill. I freeze in place, unsure who ventures this far up the mountain. Having just settled my heart, my pulse pounds loud in my ears again. I reach for the dagger sheathed at my hip and crouch behind a thicket of brush.

"The king's mages patrol the perimeter with the advance party," a male voice says.

Four riders appear on horseback wearing blue and gray, the Penyasegat colors. Niklau's soldiers. How far had the army advanced?

"I wish we'd get a mage to patrol with us," a second voice responds. "What are we supposed to do if we come across a dragon?"

"Nothing. We'd be dead before we saw it."

"Have you ever seen a dragon?"

"Not a live one."

I limp out from behind the thicket. I must look like death. Hair unbound and wild. Though my clothes are mended, they're disheveled.

"Your Highness," the first voice says when he spots me, and they lower their swords and dismount.

I limp toward them, keeping my back straight. They sink to their knees, but the stout soldier rises quickly and holds his arms up for me to take or fall into.

"How is it that you are so far up the mountain face?" I ask the scouts, taking an offered arm. My hands shake. From fear? Relief? How close to the peak is his army? Where are my men?

"Thank the gods you're here. When you were taken, King Niklau pressed the army to ride through the night. We rode for a day and a night," another soldier with a generous grin and a scar over one eye answers.

"The troops?" I ask, forcing the quiver out of my voice. I swallow the hard lump that's formed in my throat and ignore the ache in my chest as I focus on the soldier's updates.

"Both armies are still setting up camp," the stout soldier adds. "We are one of the many patrols scouting the perimeter and the surrounding terrain." He lifts me, and before I can protest, he seats me on his mount.

I'd been inside the mountain for almost two days. I glance up toward the peaks, but they are shrouded within the cloud bank. What happened to my mare? I didn't think dracs could keep horses on the rocky peaks. Would they eat her? Arik wouldn't let that happen, would he? Would she find her way home? I shudder in the saddle, struggling to keep the chill from entering me.

We ride perpendicular to the slope. The troops have advanced further than I expected.

"The king is mounting an invasion of the dragon lands to rescue you," the scarred soldier tells me as he drapes his cloak over my shoulders. They all exchange looks, smiling widely. They're pleased with themselves.

"Take me to Niklau," I say, ignoring their self-satisfied expressions. The stout solder registers my closed expression, and his smile disappears.

I will correct Niklau's assumptions at the first opportunity.

Within minutes, we enter the Penyasegat camp. The dragon deposited me close without being detected. I'd been so scared for Arik and his kind. Now I see it's my people I should be worried about. Dracs have always had the advantage. The armies would never see the dragons coming.

The scout rides through the camp. As we pass a clearing in the center of several tents, I take stock of my surroundings. There is a blacksmith and a leathersmith. There are men and women, some dressed in soldiers' uniforms and others in farming clothes, all wearing some article of blue—ribbons, scarves, sashes, armbands.

A knot in my belly tightens. This is a well-organized army, establishing itself for a long campaign. Where are my father's troops? They'd only had three days to rally.

We arrive at a large tent with banners bearing the Penyasegat colors. Niklau emerges with three guards—two men and a woman, dressed in blue robes. All three wear matching badges—a staff engulfed in flames. His mages.

"You have a team of mages," I say by way of greeting, unable to think of anything else.

"My secret weapon," he says with a proud smile.

Weapon?

He helps me down and pulls me toward a group of soldiers standing around a fire.

When I stumble, one of the scouts calls after us. "Your Highness, she's injured."

Niklau looks back at me, slowing his step, but he doesn't offer assistance.

"You've returned to us," he says over his shoulder. "We were about to launch a mountain offensive. How did you escape?"

"I was released," I say.

"Come." He barely listens as he pulls me toward an audience. "The people will be relieved to see you've returned."

We approach a group of Penyasegat soldiers milling around the fire. A half dozen blue-robed individuals stand among them. How many mages has he conscripted?

"The princess is back." Niklau's announcement stops conversation, and more soldiers gather round us.

The people cheer, but he holds his hands up to quiet their enthusiastic shouts.

Quint arrives on horseback and dismounts with a spry flourish, easing my tension at being surrounded by Niklau's soldiers and mages.

Quint stands behind me as Niklau continues to address his people. "Your Highness," Quint says in a low voice at my ear. "We were so worried."

I'm filthy. My ankle hurts. I smell Arik on my skin. Parading around is the last thing I want. I need to be briefed by my chief marshal before making a public spectacle, but Niklau likes an audience. My nerves are too frayed for diplomacy. I turn and send Quint a look, beseeching him to help me escape. To diffuse the escalating zeal.

"Her return," Niklau is saying, "clears the way for us to advance on the dragon hordes."

My head whips around to look at him. "What?"

"We will advance to take our revenge," he calls to his soldiers, "while they least expect it."

Revenge? Niklau told us his purpose here was to negotiate with the dragon keepers. Our goal had never been vengeance.

He calls on the chief marshal of his own troops. "Have we coordinated our forces?"

"Aye, sir."

The mages stand at attention with the troops, prepared to assist.

"We don't need vengeance," I call out, unable to gather my thoughts. If only Niklau had spoken with me in private. "The dragon keepers did not abduct me. It is I who sought them out."

Niklau holds up a hand to quiet his people. "What is it you say, Princess?"

"I went to the drac—the dragon keepers." There's a disquieting murmur in the crowd. "To negotiate," I add quickly.

"You betray our people in sympathy with the keepers of those foul beasts."

"No!" Shaken by the accusation, I manage to keep my voice steady. "Of course not."

Niklau interrupts me. "You abandoned your people on the eve of war to warn the enemy."

His rhetoric stirs the crowd further.

"With all the death the dragons have brought with them—"

"What death? A few sheep?" I ask, but my words are drowned by the shouting. All this over livestock?

"They threaten our livelihoods, kill our people, burn our crops, and eat our livestock. What happens when they start taking children?"

The falsehoods stagger me.

One man roars in anger. Another calls out, "We must stop them!"

Panic replaces my exhaustion. I turn to Quint, confusion clear on his face, he looks at me then at the crowd, his intent clear. He's calculating our escape route.

Niklau incites the crowd further until they advance on me.

"I was not warning them," I shout, even though it's a lie. "I was negotiating." I try to convince the crowd, but they're disturbed beyond reasoning.

"My princess, that is what we have come to do," says Niklau with a calculated coolness.

"With an army?" I shout, my nerves fraying and my composure slipping, but my voice is lost amid excitable calls for justice.

Someone from the crowd shouts, "Traitor!"

Niklau pulls me away. My injured foot twists beneath me, and I fall. The crowd cheers. Quint moves to help me, but Niklau hoists me up roughly and drags me the hundred yards or so back to his tent.

Quint follows us, his face a contorted mask of indignation, but Niklau's chief of arms prevents him from approaching the king. The three mages also step in, forming a barrier between Quint and me. The king enters his tent, and I follow behind, boxed in by his mages.

The spacious tent allows us all entry. He pushes me toward a brazier in the center of the room and forces me to my knees on the plush carpet.

Niklau swings around and nods to his mages. The shortest of them approaches Quint and blows a green dust in his face. Before my eyes, he goes slack and collapses to the ground in an indelicate heap.

My body numbs from shock.

"What is happening?" I ask as something cold and hard clamps around my ankle. An iron cuff connected with a chain to a spike in the ground at the center of the tent.

"Leave us," he tells the others. "Come back for the marshal's body after dark. Spread the word that the princess is a traitor and explain that she's warned the keepers. Advise Devantdemar's chief marshal's second that he should prepare to receive me. And prepare half our camp to return to Devantdemar. The Devantdemar forces will continue their advance on the dragon keep."

His instructions are so precise and methodical, he can't have devised them in the moment.

He turns to his chief of arms. "You will lead the Penyasegat forces to occupy Devantdemar. We cannot ally ourselves with a kingdom that would defend these animals."

"Aye, Your Highness." The chief of arms bows to his king and retreats.

I rise, my muddled brain taking in everything from the last few minutes. My eyes land on Quint, slumped by the entrance of the tent, eyes open and vacant. His skin is grayish, almost blackening, and a green foam coats his lips and drizzles down his cheek. Dead. My heart leaps forward, and my body goes to follow, but Niklau holds me back.

"Thank you, Princess," he says with a menacing smirk.

Had Niklau been planning this all along? I spy the lush space. It's comfortable. Enough for a long campaign. There's a trunk of clothes, a copper tub, and an ornamental screen that shields his bedding.

Niklau grabs my jaw, his fingers sinking into my flesh, and forces me down to the carpet. As harshly as Arik had gripped me, he'd never hurt me. This, though, from Niklau, is meant to hurt.

"You've done me a favor, Princess."

"You're twisting everything. Devantdemar is not allied with anyone."

"You defend the keepers."

"They have done nothing to warrant an assault. They've stolen a few sheep. Would you slaughter a den of wolves—"

"Yes. Yes, I would."

"Our kingdoms will not be united."

He smirks at that.

"That was never your intention," I say, comprehending. His plan goes far beyond dragon magic.

He grips my upper arm and hauls me up, not allowing me to gain my footing. He drags me behind the screen and throws me onto his cot, the long chain still shackling me to the ground. "I don't need a Devantdemar wench for a wife, but I'll accept a mistress."

When he moves to grab me, I roll onto my back and kick him in the stomach. Luckily, he clamped my injured ankle in the manacle, leaving my uninjured foot free.

He takes my blow, laughing, and launches himself at me. He sweeps my leg aside and backhands me, catching me across the cheek and eye. I don't feel the strike. I'm numb. All I can think about is keeping him off me.

I reach for the ground on the far side of the cot, looking for anything to use as a weapon. I latch onto the first thing I touch, swinging back and catching his jaw with the reinforced heel of a riding boot.

He's thrown back a few steps but recovers quickly and grabs my leg to drag me off the cot. On the ground, he presses one knee hard on my chest. I feel a pop and a sharp pain. The he's wrapping his gloved fingers around my throat.

"You have no allies in this camp." The pain in my chest drives all thought out of my head, and I nearly miss his words. "If you're good, I'll take you back to see your father."

He stands, lifts me by the arm, and tosses me back onto the bed, the impact sending a shooting pain through my whole torso.

He steps away only to return with a metal cup. Forcing my jaw open, he pours a pungent wine into my mouth. Then he closes my mouth roughly until I'm forced to swallow. When he releases me, I cough up what I can, but too soon, a heavy fog seeps into my brain.

7

An Infiltration

Arik

I stand with a dozen dracs poised to firestorm the invaders from the ridge overlooking the two camps. The heat pounding in my head and chest since I left Ophelia had abated. At least until I saw the mountainside below the tree line strewn with tents and soldiers waiting to attack my people.

If we raze the bivouacs, the disappearance of the two armies would remain a mystery. And an effective deterrent to future attacks. But the dragon keepers would be cut off from trade with the lowland kingdoms.

"She's down there, with the soldiers," Mercé tells me as steam pours from my human nostrils, contemplating a mountainside clearcutting. With her words, the rumbling rage roiling just below my chest clenches into an icy knot.

Ophelia's in the camp. In my haste to leave her, I didn't tell my dracs to return her to her home. I clench my shaking hands into fists. Like a beacon in the fog, her presence draws me out of my rageful miasma. This decides me.

It's midafternoon when I stride into the Devantdemar camp with a half dozen drac enforcers. The soldiers are distracted making camp. We keep our heads down, blending in as we observe men and women setting up tents, building cook fires, and settling in. There's an unease in the air. A sense that they're here to defend their territory yet are unaware of the exact threat. No one knows what's coming.

As we wend our way through the encampment looking for the princess's tent, the energy in the camp shifts. A ripple of disquiet reverberates over soldiers as they work in small groups. A single word catches my ear. "Traitor."

What intrigue befalls the camp?

The news is scattered, but my discomfort spikes at the rumors of the princess's betrayal. Devantdemar soldiers speak in hushed tones about their treacherous princess.

"The princess would not betray her people," one voice says.

"Maybe not, but she admitted that she went to the dragon keepers."

From another group of milling soldiers, I hear, "Niklau is taking the princess back for her father to deal with. He'll return with his army."

Bitter debates break out as her kingdom's people defend or condemn her. There is confusion and distrust among members of the camp, but I wonder if it's her people. Or are Niklau's people sowing the seeds of distrust? I suspect it's the latter. The Devantdemar people have always loved Ophelia, certain to be a compassionate ruler.

I stop to question a young man chewing on a strip of dried meat. "What is this treachery the princess is accused of?"

The young soldier's black-and-red armband displays his allegiance to Devantdemar. "The Penyasegat king is holding her in his camp. They say they found her returning from the peaks," he tells my enforcers.

My stomach lurches. *What did I send her back to?*

"I don't know about any dragon keeper alliances," he says around a mouthful of jerky. "But I know she wouldn't turn her back on her kingdom."

I spot Mercé standing among a group of soldiers sitting around a fire. The other dracs are likewise meandering through camp, gathering what information they can. When I catch Mercé's eye, she works her way over to me.

"Learn what you can," I tell her. "I'm going to find Ophelia."

Mercé sighs, reading the concern on my face. "Of course."

"Find the Devantdemar chief marshal's tent. We'll rendezvous in the area."

"Aye." She stalks toward Kaelan, another drac enforcer and her mate.

I signal two other dracs, Vix and Ferrán, to follow a distance behind me as I stalk toward Niklau's camp. We don't walk far before we spot the king himself parading through camp with a small entourage. He's heading away from his own camp, and while I'd like to go after him, his absence will make it easier to find Ophelia.

In the center of the Penyasegat camp, King Niklau's tent is easy to recognize with his banners flying high. Two guards stand sentry at the entrance, along with a man and a woman wearing blue robes in the Penyasegat colors. Mages.

My enforcers approach them. "We have a message from the dragon keeper chieftain," Vix tells them. With those words, we have the mages' full attention.

"Is King Niklau here?" Vix asks.

"You are dragon keepers?"

"We are emissaries seeking audience with your king."

The younger woman does nothing to hide the gleam in her eye. The elder guard schools his own expression, but I don't miss their exchanged glances.

The older man says, "We'll advise the king. You can wait in the tent."

I scan their faces. They show no fear even as they glance over my clanmates' shoulders to study me. Do they know we are shifters? Have they discovered our secret? A tension prickles at the back of my neck.

I meet the mages' eyes. A wave of rage crests in my chest; my fingers twinge, aching to snap necks. But we can't kill four of the king's guards in the middle of camp. We need to get inside, but we'll have to take our chances we won't be overpowered by magic upon entering the tent.

The mages gesture for us to enter, and my enforcers step aside for me to precede them. Once inside, I turn to see the tent flaps close behind the mages as Vix and Ferrán spin in coordinated moves, grab the mages at lightning speed, and snap their necks.

My dracs slide the mages' bodies behind trunks at the side of the tent. I scan the interior looking for signs of Ophelia as they decide how best to deal with the bodies.

"We should burn down the tent," Vix tells Ferrán.

"We don't want to attract attention." Ferrán says from behind me. "Not yet."

There's a spike staked into the ground, attached to a chain that runs behind an ornate screen.

"Why don't we just kill Niklau?" Vix asks Ferrán.

"We will," Ferrán, ever patient with the restless drac, answers as I walk to the privacy screen.

"I mean now," Vix says.

Ferrán answers. "We don't want an army of angry humans on our mountain. Let's send them home where they can settle their affairs away from us."

Vix. "Their affairs are our affairs as long as they're on the mountain."

Their discussion becomes background noise as I look over the screen. My attention lands on a delicate, leather-clad leg draped out from beneath blankets with a manacle at the ankle, linked to the other end of the chain. My vision clouds and narrows on the manacled foot. A spike of pure rage lances me, and my hands shake with the overwhelming urge to rain fire over the mountainside.

"Ophelia." I force a gruff whisper though I want to roar. There's no response.

I tug at the fur thrown haphazardly over her. She's wearing the mended tunic she left my caverns in this morning, but it's covered in dirt now. She's cold to the touch. I shake her, and she moans softly.

"Water," I call to my clanmates.

Ferrán hands me a cup that I hold to her lips. She rouses groggily from a deep sleep. Drugged.

I shift her onto my lap, and she gasps, eyes opening with a start as she clutches her side. When she turns her face to mine, one eye is swollen shut. I turn her body to face me. She recoils. I hold my hands out impotently, not knowing where she hurts.

Despite her wan pallor, she still radiates light and grace. The warmth that had been absent since my father died, since I assumed the mantle of chieftain, since everything changed, fills me now. I also feel the same hard impotence I felt when my father died, watching the butchers who dismembered him. She's mine. Blind prejudice colored my view of my mate even when she'd given herself wholly to me.

Guilt and shame, like poisonous tendrils, coil around my guts and creep upward to wind their way around my heart. I'd been a fool to turn my back on her. To not seek her counsel.

"Drink," I tell her.

A voice from the tent entrance says, "What's going on here?"

In a motion almost too fast to track, Ferrán reaches the intruder before the tent flap has dropped. A third neck snaps this day.

"Wait at the entrance and dispatch the other guard when he comes to check also," I order my dracs.

Ophelia opens her good eye and tries to back away, but winces in pain.

"What is this?" I ask, cupping her chin gently.

"Niklau is calling me a traitor." Her voice slurs. "I fought him." She touches her face gingerly. "He's discrediting me because I went to warn you."

"I didn't need your warning."

"You told me that already," she says, and I remember the desolate look on her face in the caverns. With slow, deliberate movements, she stands from my lap.

"I need to leave," she says, her voice stronger.

I kneel at her feet and lower my head to blow a hot breath on the chain connected to her ankle. Then I extract a claw and wedge it into a link to pry it open. When it's free, she takes a tentative step. I take her elbow to steady her, but she slips from my protective hold. Razor wire tendrils tighten in my chest.

The second guard enters the tent as Ophelia limps around the screen. His gaze lands on the princess first, giving Vix the opportunity to snap a fourth neck with a swift grace.

"Why can't we just firestorm the whole camp and get rid of all these humans in one blow?"

I register momentary concern for my enforcer's bloodlust, until I catch Ferrán rolling his eyes.

He tells Vix, "We do not kill indiscriminately. We are not monsters."

I interrupt their debate. "Give me one of the mage robes. And put them on."

"Except mages." Ferrán hurries to fetch a robe from one mage and hands it to me. "Mages we do kill indiscriminately."

Vix, the shorter of the two enforcers, dons the other robe.

I want to shift into my dragon form and unleash a gale of flames across this camp. But these are Ophelia's people. Deception has led them here. Ferrán is correct. We do not bloodshed indiscriminately. We have lived in peace with humans for generations. Keeping our true nature a secret has ensured that peace. Her people are concerned for her, and many do not believe that she would betray them. The push to get to the mountain and claim magic is driven by Niklau's machinations. Slaughtering the humans would bring war.

I keep my head for the moment. To rain fury on the humans would only result in suffering to her kind and mine. As it has in the past.

Ophelia

Arik envelopes me in a blue robe and draws the hood up over my head. A shiver runs up my arm and through my body when he reaches for me, but I step away again. I'm not scared of him. I know he wouldn't hurt me physically. But he hurt my heart. It's not physical pain that has me wary. It's the fear that I would let him hurt me again just to feel his hands on me once more.

"Did you find Quint? My chief marshal?"

"No. Just you."

I resolve to send scouts to find Quint's body once we're out of Niklau's camp.

We exit unseen and move around to the back of the tent. Arik leads me on a circuitous route in the opposite direction from where I had entered camp this morning. At least, I believe it was this morning. The sun has dipped behind the peaks, so I must have slept for most of the day.

Our pace is slow as I limp through camp with Arik at my side, one blue-robed drac in front of us and the other trailing behind us. People look at us as we pass, but the hooded mage robes obscuring mine and the dracs' faces allow us unfettered passage.

As we walk, Arik reports on my purported treachery and the whisper campaign against me. My mind is still racing to catch up when he suggests we start our own. I agree, my thoughts too muddled to devise another plan. He dispatches his dracs to spread the word in my camp that I'm no traitor and that Niklau is planning a siege of Devantdemar, using me as leverage. A good strategy—telling the truth.

"Why are you here?" My question escapes my tumultuous thoughts before I can call it back, but after the way he dismissed me, I can't understand why he's come now. *I'd have given up everything for you. I'd have climbed your peaks to follow you and leaped off the cliffs to stay with you. But you left without a word. I thought you were mine, and even if I was never yours, I'd have been your ally.*

"I heard talk in your camp."

"You were spying." Without turning to him, I ask, "How is it with all your spies, that you didn't anticipate Niklau's attack?" Seeing as he's been in both our castles all along, I welcome the bitterness that fills my chest and wraps around my heart.

"We did," he says. His stride doesn't falter, although he walks slowly to accommodate my slow pace. "We've been waiting for his army."

My step falters. "You were waiting for us." I utter the realization out loud. Of course. The dracs would wipe away the armies here, far from the villages. Where humans transgress on them. As the humans killed the dragons when they transgressed on human lands. It's an elegant, clean, and balanced retribution.

"Aye. But they accuse you of betraying your people. I know that's not true, so I came to get you."

"How honorable," I mutter under my breath, but he hears me.

"You need to leave with me."

"I need to see my chief marshal."

"He's dead."

"I know." I swallow hard around the lump in my throat. "I watched them kill Quint. His second will assume the post. I want to consult—"

Arik takes my elbow and, before I can pull away, pulls me behind a tent. He gestures uphill to where Niklau and his entourage are riding through camp, rows from where we stand.

"We need to go. They're about to discover you're gone." Gripping my arm firmly, he guides me downslope toward the edge of the camp. "Let's get you to safety."

"We'll have to come back," I say. "I need to talk with Kerik. He'll be the new chief marshal."

"Soon. For now, I'm taking you out of here. I need you safe."

I scoff at that, and his jaw clenches. But when his gaze lands on mine, the hardness is gone. His mercurial moods are as spectacular as his shifter form. I meet his gaze, forcing logic to contain my reaching heart. *You are disposable for this dragon. Don't forget that this time.*

8

A Drac Clan

Ophelia

The sun is behind the mountains by the time we reach the outer perimeter of the camp. Arik wraps his fingers around my arm, just above the elbow. His touch is warm and possessive. As it always was. I don't pull away this time. *Helping me walk,* I tell myself.

"Niklau told your new chief marshal that they are taking you to your father," Arik tells me when we're well beyond the camp boundary. "Niklau is sending his forces back to your lands. He means to take your kingdom."

I stop and look up into his face. Had that been Niklau's plan all along? Have we been so naive?

"I need to speak to my father," I say. My heart stutters beneath Arik's fathomless black eyes. The same penetrating eyes I used to lose myself in. I turn away. "I need a horse."

Arik dips and slides one arm behind my back and the other behind my legs, scooping me up. I wince and grip my side.

"You're in pain," he says through his clenched teeth.

I close my eyes, holding myself stiff in his arms. I am in pain. It hurts to walk. It hurts to breathe. It hurts to think, but I need to be practical. His hard body pressed to my side and strong arms supporting me make me want to slump against him and rest. Yet I hold firm.

He picks up his pace and walks perpendicular to the slope. Once we're out of sight of the camp, he says, "I'll take you to see your father."

"Where is Serendipity?"

"She's safe. We'll bring her down the mountain when this is over."

Without another word, he shifts into his dragon form in two steps and lifts us into the air. He cradles me in blue-and-black scaly forelegs that are gentler than the massive claws appear. He coasts low above the tree line away from the camps' line of sight to avoid being seen by any soldiers. Just as it once did, the heat from his body keeps me warm despite the whipping winds. I resist the temptation to feel safe in his arms.

Arik

The vibrant smile she'd given me in the cave is gone. Even kneeling and chained on the floor in the dark, she had radiated joy when she heard my voice. From the way she holds herself rigid now, I can tell I squashed that joy. My guts contract into a tight knot, aching to draw her smile out again.

I had watched her these two long years, the way she interacted with others. A gracious diplomat who wears many masks, yet she'd never worn a mask with me. Not until now. The knot in my belly that had been cinching since I sent her away this morning tightens. Everything in me was rebelling as I walked away, ignoring the aching inside me. Ignoring her.

I'd abandoned Ophelia. Then when she thought we might be reunited, I rubbed that abandonment in her face. She had kept our drac secrets. She was the loyal one. It was I who'd failed our bond.

I cradle her firmly against my body to keep her from jostling in flight.

I don't deserve her, but she's mine. I have to show her I can be a worthy mate.

Ophelia

The moon shines bright, unlike all the nights Arik visited me. Back when he loved me. For two years, I waited on each new moon for him. All the while he hated me for what humans had done to his father and his clanspeople. Tonight, his dragon wings shine in the moonlight.

I keep my breaths shallow. Arik's grip is firm and secure, my body braced tight, allowing me to settle into the persistent ache. If my heart pounds any harder, it will bruise my ribs from the inside. I'm not sure where the physical pain from Niklau's abuse ends and the pain in my heart begins.

Coming in low, Arik enters the palace grounds through the garden terraces, which he knows well from our moonless rendezvous. He shifts as we land in the shadows and sets me down gently. We enter the castle through the garden gate. When he takes the lead, I realize he knows his way around. He's been here, inside my home.

Had he been watching me? Of course not. He'd been spying on my father and my people The forgotten lump in my throat throbs back to life.

I stop when I become dizzy from my shallow breathing. Arik reaches for me as I lean against the wall, but I put my hand up. His jaw tightens as he scrutinizes my face. Then I remind myself that his concern for me is my own wishful fancy. I take as deep a breath as my battered chest allows.

We reach my father's study. Soft light flickers under the door. I open it slowly and look through the gap.

"Father," I call from the entrance when I see him sitting in the firelight of the hearth. He's alone. "Where are your advisors?"

He rushes over. "Where have you been, Ophelia? Look at you."

I put my hands up to stop him when he moves to wrap his arms around me. Arik steps between us protectively, and Father's forehead scrunches with blatant curiosity.

"We've been worried," he says. He keeps his arms open, raising his hands to my face. He studies my swollen eye, which must be black now. But he doesn't touch the tender skin, thankfully.

"I went to the dragon keep."

"Have you lost your senses? Did they do this to you?"

"No, Father." Rushing ahead, I don't give myself the chance to blush at the memory of what I had done at the dragon keep. "Niklau did this. And yes, Father. I am incensed. We cannot attack the… the dragon keepers to kill and steal from them."

"But the magic, Ophelia."

The heat radiating off Arik rises. I resist looking at him. Would he hurt my father?

"You would destroy majestic creatures for magic?"

"No, Ophelia. I would destroy majestic creatures to protect our kingdom from Niklau. The only way to do that is to cultivate magic and align ourselves with him until the time comes when we must defend ourselves against him."

"You promised me to him." My voice rises an octave. That he would go back on his word and offer me as a buffer to Niklau's ambitions out of fear.

"With you at his side, his ambitions would be tempered. United through marriage, he would not turn his sights on Devantdemar as a territory. Or if he tried, you would be there to control him. That would give us time to bolster our defenses."

"You used me as a pawn?" My voice is barely above a whisper. Pure stubbornness keeps me from slumping against Arik.

"You are a natural leader," he says, his tone gentle. "You would maintain peace, and you would stay abreast of their discoveries in magic."

"Father, I would not have survived a year of marriage at his side."

My father walks to the windows overlooking the palace grounds and the fields beyond the walls to the mountains. "You would, Daughter. You are a force of nature and a true leader. I don't fear for you."

I don't bother arguing. There's no time. I continue with my news. "He killed Quint."

His head snaps around. "What? How?"

"Magic." I turn away, not wanting to condemn my father with a look. "That's not all. His army is returning to advance on Devantdemar. He means to take our city."

"Returning? And our soldiers?"

"They've been ordered to stay in the mountains." Arik speaks for the first time. "Niklau's force will arrive by morning. He'll approach the castle expecting you to welcome him. Especially if he is returning with Ophelia. He believes it will be a small matter to commandeer the castle while your army remains in the mountains. Then he'll rejoin your troops for the dragon keep."

"It would be a small matter with our soldiers gone. Very canny."

Father looks out the window, peering deep into the night. Probably looking for signs of life in the foothills.

"I will order our soldiers back," I say. "You must call in the townsfolk and villagers and keep our gates closed."

"We will secure the castle. How will you return in time? And who is this you travel with?"

"Father, this is chieftain Arik of the dragon keepers. We will return by dragon."

The king raises his chin in agreement to the chieftain, who returns the gesture. "By dragon?" My father studies Arik a moment before asking, "We are allied then?"

I say, "Until they remove the threat of Niklau. When they'll return to the mountains. And on the condition that we agree to leave off any plans of acquiring magic. They owe us no allegiance."

The lump in my throat expands into my chest. I don't look to Arik for confirmation.

"It is generous of them," I add, "considering our soldiers are camped at their door."

My father looks over my shoulder to the chieftain. "You are the chieftain now. Your father is gone?"

Arik jerks his chin.

"I met him, your father. When I was crowned," he says. "He was an impressive man. I'm sorry to hear of his passing."

Arik's jaw clenches. I don't remark that my father attended the celebration of his destruction. The heat in my father's study rises, but when Arik's gaze shifts to me, his eyes are ice.

Arik reaches for my elbow. This time, I allow the touch, and for a moment I imagine the tension in his shoulders eases. "We must go."

"Where?" my father asks, frowning.

"To check on our army," I say.

"I will go in your stead. You need to stay and heal. What's happened to your foot?" I still have an iron cuff with a few trailing links cuffed to the outside of my boot.

"She'll be fine." Arik brooks no discussion. "We have healers to treat her wounds. We'll return in the morning with reinforcements to deal with Niklau."

My father must see something in Arik he trusts because he doesn't argue.

"Father, if you put the orders in a writ for our new chief marshal, Kerik, he won't question our allegiance."

"Of course." Father turns to his desk and scratches out the order on a piece of parchment. He melts wax and stamps the seal with his ring. After blowing on it, he hands it to me.

Before I turn to leave, my father holds both hands out to Arik, who surprises me by taking my father's smaller hands in his. Father's hands are much older and frailer than I remember.

"Please keep her safe," my father says. "And make sure she rests. She needs to heal."

Arik answers, "On my honor."

I raise a brow at that as I turn to stalk out, and Arik smirks. I ignore how the playful smile conjures up memories of playing naked with him on moonless nights.

Arik

I launch us into the air, holding Ophelia firmly against me to keep her still. She curls into me. She's exhausted—the only reason she's allowed herself to settle into my hold. Though her eyes are getting heavy, she fights to stay awake. I argued that we should go directly to the drac healer, but she insists on speaking with her new chief marshal first. The troops need to mobilize if they are to arrive in time to defend the castle.

Despite her exhaustion, and the momentary wave of dizziness, she fights to stay upright when we land. Once I shift back into my human form under the cover of the trees, she marches, limping, into her people's camp. We make our way through camp in search of the command tent, her stride purposeful despite her limp. Her father is right—she is a force of nature.

I spot Vix and Ferrán loitering in the vicinity. They've shed the mage robes. They meet my gaze with a warning look, then saunter over to join us, though they keep their distance. I draw Ophelia's attention to Mercé and Kaelan sitting with another group of soldiers nearby. They've been observing Niklau's tent since we left. The sun has set and many fires have been built up, perhaps to ward off the unsettling pall creeping over the camp.

We approach the tent in time to meet the two mages that emerge. One of them hurls himself toward her when he sees Ophelia's blue robe. I pull her away as Ferrán cuts in front of the mage in one fluid motion, just as a cloud of green dust wafts into the air around his face. Ferrán buckles and drops to the ground.

I look to the other mage, but Mercé is standing where he had been a moment before, the mage now slumped at her feet. Vix is at the remaining mage's side a moment too late. In a blink, Devantdemar's new chief marshal is already pulling his blade out of the mage's back. The mage slumps to the ground in a heap next to her brethren. With my focus on putting myself between Ophelia and the threat, I didn't see the chief marshal exit the tent behind the mages.

I move without thought, and Ophelia is in my arms, shielded from toxic potions and deadly fists. But she's gripping her dagger and elbowing herself from my grip.

"Your Highness," the new chief marshal says and drops his head in a bow.

"Is he dead?" she asks, peering around me at Ferrán. She struggles to stand upright with her hand braced against her side, but her voice is strong. I want to sweep her away from this place, but the determination on her face grounds me. Her priority right now is her people.

Vix kneels next to Ferrán's body, whose face is dusted with the green powder.

"Be careful of the dust," Ophelia calls to them over my shoulder. "That's how they killed Quint."

"He's breathing," Vix says as he kneels next to him.

"Take him home," I order my dracs.

Mercé organizes our clanmates. "Get a blanket from the tent. Don't touch the dust. Get him to Rowena."

Ophelia slips out of my arms and stands up straight, pulling her robes tight around her. "That powder could level an army."

"It's how they bring down dragons," I tell her. "The mages use our magic to boost the potency of natural toxins."

"Kerik," Ophelia says to her chief marshal.

I move in front of her as the marshal approaches her, but Ophelia steps around me as he bows low. "Your Highness. I don't believe a word of what they said. Niklau's first chief of arms is inside."

Chief Marshal Kerik gestures for Ophelia to proceed inside, but I hold her back. Kaelan enters the tent as Kerik explains, "He's dead. I was able to take him down during the scuffle."

Kaelan exits the tent and gives me a nod of assent. I lead Ophelia in.

Our meeting is quick. Ophelia hands Kerik her father's writ and explains Niklau's plans.

"I suspected there was more to his scheme, but I didn't imagine that he would be so bold as to stage an overthrow," Kerik says.

"You will have reinforcements by morning," I tell the head of Ophelia's army. "Hold in the foothills until you see Ophelia meet Niklau. Then advance. Direct troops to hold the passage through the mountains as well."

Kerik looks to Ophelia for confirmation. Her face is wan, and shadows haunt her eyes. Wordlessly, she assents with a jerk of her chin.

"You are coming as well?" Kerik asks Ophelia, taking in her face and her posture. He gestures for her to take a seat.

Ophelia's voice is soft, lacking the assertive tone I'm accustomed to. It's almost a whisper. "Yes, I will be there."

I want to pull her against me, but I suspect she has a broken rib. Besides, my proud princess would not permit herself to be carried off in front of her people.

"We leave you now to organize your men," I tell Kerik, meeting Ophelia's gaze. She agrees with a simple tilt of her chin, another sign of her exhaustion. "I'll leave dragon keepers with you for support and to serve as messengers if necessary."

"Yes, sir," he says to me, looking to Ophelia for confirmation.

She nods and smiles weakly.

"Your Highness, if I may ask, where are the dragons?"

With a smile, I answer for her. "They are camouflaged in the trees."

His shoulders slump, but he nods in acknowledgment. He's curious about the legendary beasts. Tomorrow, he will see dragons.

Ophelia

It takes all my energy to stand. I brace myself against the sharp pain shooting up my side as I straighten. It's bad enough that my people must see me limping with my face battered. They need not know my body is broken inside too.

Arik holds the flap of the tent open for me and takes my elbow as we enter the night. I pull my arm from his and readjust to grip his upper arm. He holds firm, taking the weight I lean on him. I leave my hood off, waving and smiling as we walk by soldiers preparing for their descent. Voices hush and heads dip in respectful bows as we stride out of camp. Word has spread of Niklau's actions. Kerik will rally the troops for the return down the mountain. For now, it's enough to appear before them.

I don't look back when we leave camp, but I trust that we're out of sight of my people when Arik scoops me into his arms. A whimper escapes me, but I'm too tired to protest. I sink into his warm embrace.

I wake when I feel us landing, Arik's claws shifting into strong arms and hands beneath me.

9

A Healing Princess

Ophelia

We arrive at the entrance of a small cavern at the base of a ravine between two peaks at the mountaintop. There's a small lake where mountain goats graze nearby. Dragons ride air currents overhead, and men and women on the ground tend to the goats. One drac man works leather at another cave entrance, several paces away along the ravine wall.

Arik doesn't put me down, even when a woman with long, flowing red hair hurries from the cave entrance. "Vix told me you were coming," she says by way of greeting.

"Princess, this is Rowena. Our clan healer."

The woman beams at me as Arik introduces her.

"A healer?" I ask, confused. "I thought dracs healed themselves."

"We do, but there are some things that need help. And there are humans that live among us." Rowena's eyes are kind, and her smile is warm and sympathetic. "Look at you, poor dear. You have had a day. Let's set you right."

She's young to be a healer, but her confidence allays any doubts. Then I remember she could be as old as Arik, who is over a century old.

The entrance opens to a large chamber with an enormous hearth at the wall near the entrance.

"This cave has been the healer's workshop for generations," Arik says. "It's isolated from the central drac lair. She and her mate live nearby so she can be close to treat the ill or injured."

Shelves are mounted against almost every wall, storing jars full of liquids and dried plants, books and scrolls, containers of every shape and material, and an assortment of curiosities. At the center of the room is a workbench. Beyond that, a bed is covered with soft-looking furs, too inviting for simply tending to patients. To the left of the fireplace, thickly padded chairs and a settee are positioned out of the way of traffic but close enough to benefit from the heat of the hearth. Despite the rock walls, cluttered furnishings, busy shelves, and torchlight, the cave is cozy and warm.

"Lay her on the bed," Rowena tells Arik.

He does, then sits next to me with his hand resting on my hip.

"Give her some room to breathe, Arik. You're worse than my Naith." Turning to me, Rowena adds, "These drac boys are so clingy, I wonder how they ever learn to fly."

Arik shifts to the foot of the bed with a grumble, moving his hand to rest on my shin. I almost laugh but catch myself before I trigger an organ-piercing pinch in my side.

"How is Ferrán?" I ask. "They brought him here, didn't they?"

"Aye, Princess. He's well. I sent him home to sleep off the toxin in his own bed. The mages are using hemlock enhanced with magic to increase its efficacy and delivery. Quite ingenious, the dirty curs. It's not deadly to dragons though. It just puts them to sleep. That's the only way they can harvest our magic."

"To sleep?" I ask as she rubs an aromatic ointment over my bruised eyelid and cheek with gentle fingers.

She blows on my face. There is a warm tingling sensation, then the tight stretch of skin. The throb surrounding my eye eases.

"Our magic leaves us when we die, Princess. Mages can only harvest our dragon magic while we're alive."

"What?" The question comes out on a gasp, and I catch Arik giving Rowena a disapproving look.

"She must understand what's happening, Arik. She's a leader."

Not meeting Arik's gaze, I ask, "How do mages harvest magic? How do they even know to?"

"They tap into their own magic to draw naturally flowing magic into themselves. All living things have magic. It's the spark of life. Some humans, usually healers, have an instinct for it."

"But how do they know how to get more?" I ask with a tone more clipped than I intend, but Rowena's patient smile is understanding.

"It's all scribed. Books and scrolls in your libraries" She gestures to the walls. "Over the years, we've appropriated all the books from the lowlanders' libraries. We thought we'd gotten all the records."

The news lands like a boulder in the room. They'd been spying and stealing from us for decades. Centuries. It's the only way they could control knowledge of their shifter identity.

As a human, I shouldn't know this, of course, but it stings that it's a secret he kept from me.

Arik glowers at Rowena.

"Fft. Arik, you've brought her here." She glowers playfully back at him. "There's obviously trust. Don't give me that cranky look."

Turning to me, she says, "Princess, you have to understand, dracs only want peace. Confiscating a few books is the best of all possible solutions. The alternative is too extreme to consider. Other dragon clans manage human populations more ruthlessly. But we choose to coexist with your kingdoms."

Arik never told me any of this. *How little I know about him.*

I say nothing else as Arik and Rowena watch me intently. When I open my now-healed eye, Arik releases a long, slow breath.

"Better?" he asks.

I reach up to touch my cheek below my eye. It's still tender, but even under the gentle prodding of my fingers, the pain is dull. "Yes."

"What else?" Rowena asks. "You were holding your side when you came in."

"Broken ribs, I think," Arik answers.

I relax back, resting my hand on my rib cage.

"This has seen better days." She slices my tunic open from hem to collar with a sharp blade.

My binding cloth was rendered useless when Arik slashed it off my body in the dungeons, so I wear nothing under my tunic. When she opens it and reveals my breasts, I become self-conscious as my nipples pebble in the chill.

Arik

The inky black stain covering Ophelia's side and lower breast has me growling. Rowena lets out an audible breath. *What did Niklau do to her?*

"This looks like it hurts, you poor dear." Rowena rests her hands on Ophelia's ribcage and probes gently. Ophelia winces in response each time Rowena finds a tender spot. "I'm sorry, Princess. There's a broken rib here. Two, maybe. How did you do this?"

"He kneeled down on me." Ophelia's voice is soft. Distant. Her head is back, eyes closed, on the verge of losing her fight with unconsciousness.

"I'm going to give you something to help you sleep, but it looks like you may not need it."

I run my thumb over the smaller bruises on her hips. Rowena gives me a knowing look, but I can't bring myself to regret marking her. Soon my marks will be permanent. If I can win her back.

Ophelia's next words bring me to the present. "I need to return to confer with my chief marshal."

"I'm afraid you're not going anywhere tonight," Rowena responds before I can. "You'll need to rest to heal completely." She hands her patient a cup of sweet-smelling herbal tea.

"We have time," I say to reassure her. "It's early yet. We've left a few dracs there to assist and to convey messages. It will take us moments to reach the castle before Niklau arrives at its walls. You have the remainder of the night to rest." I have no intention of trying to hold her back. If she's ever going to trust me again, she needs my backing, not my control.

Appeased, Ophelia opens her eyes and raises her head to sip the tea.

"This will help you heal on the inside," Rowena says. "It's not just a sleeping draught." She turns to me. "Let Ophelia heal. She'll sleep a while, and she's fine with me. Come back for her later."

"I'm staying with her."

Rowena must read my offended expression because she smirks as she rubs ointment over Ophelia's ribcage. Ophelia flinches.

I snatch the bowl out of Rowena's hands and say, "I'll do it."

"Of course." Rowena chuckles. "Make sure to blow on her skin when you finish. That's the magic that catalyzes the healing."

Rowena steps away to stir a pot of stew simmering on the fire. I apply ointment to the bruised area as Ophelia holds her breath. When I smooth the balm over the underpart of her breast, her nipple puckers. I glance at her face, and she's biting her lower lip. I blow on her side and breast.

A soft cloth is dropped carefully over her glorious breasts, hiding them from me.

"Rest, Arik. She needs rest." Rowena's scolding brings a smile to Ophelia's sleepy face. "Let me tend to her ankle." To Ophelia, she says, "Sleep, Princess. You are safe here. Even if our chieftain is a big muttonhead."

Her eyes closed, Ophelia chuckles softly but doesn't wince. Good. That means she's healing.

"I'll have you laughing again soon," I tell my mate.

"If I can leave her in your responsible hands, I'll go home to Naith tonight. He'll be happy."

"Thank you, Row."

Ophelia's breathing is steady. Sleeping.

"You're welcome. Arik, be careful with her. I sense grief on her. She may be strong, but she's weary. And she needs more mending than just her bones."

Rowena takes her knife and runs the blade with deft and deliberate motion along the length of Ophelia's leather breeches. I help pull the pants away, revealing strong legs, round hips, and the curls obscuring the source of my mate's scent. Rowena tugs the sheet down to Ophelia's knees to cover her.

"She's my mate," I tell Rowena, as though that excuses my lusting after the wounded woman on the bed.

"Wonderful. We'll dance to celebrate when she's awake. Right now, she needs rest."

Ophelia's peaceful slumber reassures me we can heal what's broken between us.

10

A Secret Spring

Ophelia

I awake in Arik's arms, curled into his side. I take stock of my body. My side doesn't hurt. My foot doesn't hurt. My face doesn't hurt. The absence of pain allows other sensations to surface. Warmth fills my chest. I feel protected here.

I don't trust the feeling.

Once upon a time, Arik called me his mate, then he'd disappeared from my life to foster a blinding hatred for me. He never tried to speak to me. With news of each downed dragon, my fear ratcheted to intolerable levels. For two years, I lived with the dread that the next dragon could be him. And he never came back.

Rowena's tea can't cure the hurt lingering in my heart.

Other sensations flood my awareness. My leg is draped over his, and his thick, muscular thigh is pressed against the apex of mine, the heat there undeniable. My breasts are pressed against his side, my nipples sensitive to the friction created with each breath. His cheek rests atop my head, and each exhale blows into my hair, sending tingles down my spine. His wild masculine scent envelops me.

I won't deny it. This magnificent beast can hurt me again and again, and I may keep coming back for his touch regardless.

"I can smell your cunt, and I can feel your brain working."

"What time is it?" I ask, ignoring the jolt of heat that his words ignite between my legs.

"Early yet. You've only slept a few hours. How do you feel?"

I disentangle myself to stretch, enjoying physical painlessness.

"Amazing. I feel great."

I'm unconcerned when he pulls the furs down to reveal my breasts, and his gaze caresses my body. He places a hand on my healed, unmarred ribs, his eyes staying on my breasts.

Whatever I am to this beast, I love him with the whole of my being. In this moment, I accept that this truth may be my undoing. I want to spread my legs and invite him to explore me.

Instead, I say, "I need to get cleaned up."

His thumb swipes the tight bud of my nipple, sending ripples of sensation between my legs. Heat and wetness spread between my thighs.

"I have a surprise for you," he says, raising his gaze from my breasts to meet my eyes.

He doesn't try to carry me, instead holding his hand out for me to take. I hesitate, but the thrill of touching him is too great a temptation, so I take his proffered hand. He leads me down a narrow corridor, warmer than the antechamber that is Rowena's workshop.

I follow him, admiring his lithe strides, the soft shadows in the dimly lit space highlighting the graceful sway of hard muscles and taut skin. My body remembers those curves and lines against me, around me, inside me.

We enter another chamber with a steaming, crystalline pool. The gentle rush of falling water fills the room, bathing me in calm.

"Rowena's family claimed this cavern for their workshop because of these springs." He leads me to the water's edge. "Step in, my love."

I outwardly flinch in response to the endearment. My heart swells at the warmth in his voice, yet my stomach tightens defensively. He gives my fingers a gentle squeeze. This is the drac I used to know.

The water gets deeper as I step into the darkness, and I wade out to a drac-made retaining wall. My breath catches at the black space beyond the wall. Looking down, there is only the inky shimmer of the pool below.

"The spring used to pour out into a waterfall," Arik says from behind me. "We dammed it so the healers could use the pool for healing."

"It feels wonderful," I say, soaking in the heat of the water to soothe my lingering aches.

He turns my chin to face him and says, "I'm going to wash you now." The words are soft, almost a question. The heat in his eyes asks for more.

"Please," I say, my need matching his. This may be the last time I enjoy his hands on me, and I mean to relish each touch.

I turn to survey the chasm below and push my hair back over my shoulders for him. He lathers soap into my wet locks to the sound of water gently falling. His strong fingers massage my scalp, and my muscles relax under his touch. After, he holds me and tilts me back to rinse the soap. I close my eyes and revel in the feeling of the water flowing over my scalp and his body pressed against mine. Then he drizzles oil on my head and works his fingers through the tangles in my long, wavy locks.

Without a word, he takes my hand and guides me back to where the water is waist-high, near a ledge lined with soaps and bottles. He lathers soap in his hands, and with eyes locked on mine, he rubs it over my shoulders and my front. My nipples tighten again when he lingers over my breasts.

I meet his gaze, unwilling to break his spell. His fingers are gentle compared to the last time we were together. I love everything he does to me, hard and soft. I would have been his willing play toy for always. I gird myself against the inevitable loss when he leaves me again.

If I tell him to stop, he will. But I want this. Him. Once more.

Still holding my gaze, he rubs more soap on my hips. He reaches around to my ass and lingers there, spreading my cheeks and sliding his fingers to stroke my backhole. "This is the only part of you I haven't had, and I mean to take it."

I can't help pressing back into the deliciously forbidden sensation.

"Not today," he says with a devilish smile. "But soon."

My pussy throbs, and I'm flush with liquid heat.

"Your scent is my obsession of choice."

The wall I've built separating the want of my body from the desire in my heart fractures a little at the force of his words. I don't want him to stop, but in the dungeon yesterday, his fucking was born out of spite or addiction despite hate. Yet today there is affection in his gaze.

I can fortify myself against the hurt, but his shifting moods shake my foundations.

"What's changed?" I ask, desperate to find solid ground.

"Nothing," he growls, his mouth against my ear.

The words come as a blow. He still hates me. And the solid ground slips away from beneath my feet. Stupid girl, clinging to an untethered lifeline.

His hands slide between my legs. He washes me with adept fingers, one hand stroking my folds from the front and the other teasing my ass from behind. He's driving the need in my body, despite the pain in my heart. He coaxes out more of my essence to feed his addiction. I grip his shoulders, no longer able to stand without support.

He stops abruptly, steps against me, and lifts my legs to lower us into the water, rinsing the soap from our bodies. Then he brings me to the edge of the pool, which is shallower still. He lays me at the water's edge and washes my legs, coating them with lather as he kneels between them. He raises one leg and massages every inch all the way to my toes. He repeats the process with my other leg, never taking his eyes off my pussy. It's as though he's testing his endurance. Or mine, because by the time he finishes both legs my pussy is throbbing with a need like I've never known.

If this is hatred, then I'm starving for his.

Finally, he leans in and presses into my pussy with an open-mouthed kiss that makes me gasp for air. He tongues my channel and drinks from me. With my first uninhibited moan, his fingers are inside me, his tongue flicking my clit with undeterred fervor. If my own addiction is desperate, his is driven by some otherworldly force in its relentlessness.

Before long, I'm cumming all over his face. He removes his fingers to spread my lips open and lap at me like a favorite dessert.

When he's satisfied, he reinserts his fingers to fuck me through my ebbing orgasm, my pussy walls milking his fingers, desperate for more.

Once my pulsing slows to an intermittent flutter, he slides out and climbs up my body. He kisses me generously, sharing my cum with me. My pussy clenches once more as I taste myself on his lips.

I grip him hard. "More," I beg, needing, starving for him to vanquish me. To take all his pain out on me. If not for love, then for hate.

There is no hesitation. He pushes my legs toward me, tilting my hips up, and drops into me with one hard, precise thrust. He fills me completely. I shudder under him at the blind pleasure that fills me. He's many times the thickness of his fingers, and I need it all.

"Use me," I beg, panting. "Use me like I'm your whore. Use me like you did in the dungeon."

He falters then.

I want him to purge himself of his anger. "Use me. Take out your hatred on me."

"No," he moans into my hair. "No."

He slides a hand around my thigh and under my tailbone to protect my back from the unforgiving rock floor as he cups the back of my head gently.

His thrusts are steady and measured, long and languid, as he gives me his cock in deep strokes. I welcome the slick glide of him against the lining of my channel.

I moan loudly to the rocks, and they echo back at us. "Please, harder. I need," I beg.

He lets loose, powering into me with chaotic abandon. I hold my legs open wide, my hands around my ankles, as he pounds into me.

"No," he moans again as he powers into me.

He uses me, despite his denial. I give myself completely for him to do with as he needs. I am his willing whore. As always, he awakens every base need in me.

"Ophelia," he groans as his thrusts become violent.

"Yes, Arik... Fuck... Cumming," I shout as my pussy grips him repeatedly, and I cum all over his cock.

He bucks, spending into me.

After, he doesn't stop. He slides in a few more measured strokes, mixing our fluids inside me.

He clings to me. "I'm never letting you go again."

I say nothing, lost in the promise of his words and the feeling of his skin everywhere it touches me. I don't accept that I'm his mate. He has my heart and my body, but my trust is something else.

His cock stops twitching inside me, and he rolls onto his back with me draped over his chest, cock still warming my pussy.

We lay there a long time before his words rumble through his body beneath me. "I made a terrible mistake not trusting you—and both our people suffer for it. You and I suffer for it."

I lash down the hope that flares in my chest.

"You were holding my father's dismembered claw." His voice is soft, resigned. "The man I thought you'd agreed to marry was slaughtering our young ones when they were acting with childish recklessness, because he wanted boots and potions and fancy trinkets. Those are my drac kin he's wearing. My kind's body parts he gifted to you."

I push up onto my elbows on his chest and meet his gaze. "I'm sorry," I say. The words don't capture the chasm of regret that drops out from beneath me, but it's all I have.

"A queen doesn't apologize."

"I feel your sorrow, though. Felt it then. And I'm not a queen yet."

"You will be." His lips brush mine. "Nothing has changed for me. You are my mate, but even if you weren't, I would still love you until we breathe our last. Even if it takes that long to earn your forgiveness. I love you."

That hopeful twinge perks up. The words feel true in my heart. Maybe I can't trust myself, either. My eyes stay closed.

Outside Rowena's cave, we meet Mercé and her mate, Kaelan. With them stand hundreds of dracs, many in human form and others in dragon form. Arik paces before them as men and women climb onto the backs of the dragons. The dragon keepers are riding on dragonback, so there's no need to reveal they are shifters. He has agreed to support my army in defense of the castle. But it is clear from the force of tooth, claw, and warrior he is offering more than mere support. This day, my people will witness a legion of dragons. The first time in living memory.

As I step to follow Arik, Mercé takes my arm and holds me back.

"He's a good drac, but he has a duty to his kind."

"I understand duty," I tell her. "I won't stand in the way of his."

Our kinds can't mix. At least not the rulers of enemy realms, though we played at the fantasy once. But the warning from his clanmate douses the flicker of hope I'd begun to nurse. For a fragile moment, his words wound their way into the cracks of my wall, a balm to my bruised soul. But in the early light of dawn, our horizon looks different.

Mercé steps in front of me, squaring her shoulders with mine. "That's not what I mean."

She must read my puzzled expression because she smiles at me. "He lost his father at the hands of your people. Then he had to step into his father's shoes and rule our kind on the same day. He had to put duty first. He didn't make a choice. His duty is his existence. When you become his mate, part of the clan, you become his duty as well. There is no choice about it. I just wanted you to know. He didn't choose to leave you. He accepted his duty to his drac."

"I understand." That ember of hope flares back to life like night-blooming jasmine on a moonless night. "Thank you for telling me that."

She hands me a fleece-lined leather riding coat. "A cloak will catch the wind and be a hindrance. This is better for riding the skies. It'll keep you warm."

"Thank you," I say again. My shoulders release a lingering tension at her acceptance, the drac's acceptance, as I slip my arms through the sleeves and close the fastenings.

Mercé smiles and gives my arm a gentle squeeze before climbing onto the back of her mate, the brown-and-green dragon who stands nearby.

Arik returns. "I will ride with you as chieftain of the dragon keepers. I won't shift in front of the people. But you have Vix, Kaelan, Mercé, and me as personal guard. Two dragons and two keepers. My army is yours to command."

Vix lands next to us in dragon form with a flourish, and Arik gestures for me to climb onto Vix's back. I settle into a saddle at the base of his long neck, braced with a harness across his chest and forearms. My new riding coat opens below the lowest belly fastening to cover my legs to my knees. I never needed a harness when I rode Arik, but when I rode him, I clung to his neck with both arms and legs. This more dignified configuration lets me hold on to an elongated pommel and maintain some mobility.

Arik climbs on and settles in the saddle behind me, wrapping his arms around me and pressing the front of his body flush against my back.

A silence settles over the dracs ready to take flight around me, and they turn to me expectantly.

"This is your command," Arik says in a low voice against my ear.

Arik

My princess's voice is strong as she captures the attention of my dracs and affirms our plan once more. "Our mission in the valley will be strategic. There is no question that you can wipe out a human army with one heated exhale and a flutter of wings. This is as much a show of force and as it is a diversion. Consider this an introduction."

Only the wind through the canyon competes with Ophelia's orders, our company of winged troops utter no sound as she speaks.

"The rear band will target the mages among the soldiers and dispose of them."

My dracs listen. As angry as they are at the legions from Penyasegat, there is no sport in leveling villages and laying waste to farms for us. I give her hips a squeeze.

"This display of strength and restraint will discourage future hunting of dracs."

My dracs don't even look to me for confirmation, and pride fills my chest at the natural command my mate takes of the clan we'll lead together.

II

A Battle of Dracs and Mages

Ophelia

We soar with the fleet of dragons and their riders before dawn. We circle around to approach via the southern coastline, the circuitous route in the dark camouflaging our arrival. Arik and I are ready and waiting outside the city gates when Niklau and his army, which has marched through the night, arrive.

The dragon force at our back numbers one hundred dragons with their riders. The army of colorful winged beasts are poised with a lethal grace. The riders could shift into dragons as well, potentially doubling their numbers, though the dracs do not intend to reveal themselves today. As far as the Devantdemar and Penyasegat people are aware, they are facing the dragon keeper clan riding trained dragons.

Another one hundred dragons without riders flank Niklau's soldiers, bringing the number to about three hundred dracs. Almost every able-bodied adult dragon had come to avenge the deaths of their chieftain and loved ones.

The most Niklau can hope for is to escape with his life, but Arik wants those mages eradicated. Retreat is not an option.

When Niklau breaks free of the line to approach us, I call out, "If I am hurt, you and your people will be roasted alive."

Although there is rumbling among the Penyasegat crowd at that, the troops are silent. No doubt struck silent by the sight of the lethal army of wings, teeth, and claws poised to attack.

"Princess, you did ally yourself with the dragon keepers. Tsk on you for lying. I misjudged your allegiances."

"I have no influence. I'm simply not engaging in the slaughter of their dragons."

Fury radiates off Vix's body and ripples through my body. I vaguely wonder if the dragon won't rear back and crispify Niklau where he stands.

Arik presses his body against my back. "Steady," he croons. I'm not sure if he's reassuring me or calming Vix.

I resist the urge to look to the skies when I see movement in the distance.

"So what are we doing here, Your Highness?"

Though Niklau's confidence unnerves me, my voice is steady. "You'll return home and leave our lands. And you'll cease felling dragons."

He doesn't respond, and I continue speaking, my goal not to extract empty promises but to keep his eyes trained on me. "Our betrothal contract is dissolved."

Niklau laughs at that.

"We will close the passage through the mountain pass," I say when he's finished.

Niklau scoffs. "That's ridiculous. You need that passage for trade."

"The dragon keepers have agreed to patrol the passage."

"So you are allied, Ophelia?"

His condescending use of my first name is my only hint he's unnerved.

A collective gasp surges from the rear of the opposing forces.

I keep my eyes trained on Niklau. "We are."

With those words, fourteen dracs come into view, coasting low over the assembled forces from the rear in a staggered formation. I hear a few isolated screams through the unsettling silence that grips the Penyasegat army as the dragons pass overhead. I keep my gaze locked with Niklau's. The twitch in his cheek is the only sign that he hears the murmuring behind him. Though he doesn't turn to look, probably confident in his mages. Until now he'd only seen young dragons and one aging one.

The dragons advance on the front line fast. The two in the lead snatch up the mages at Niklau's side—including the one who killed Quint. Gripped by their upper arms, they are unable to toss their toxic dust into the dragons' faces.

Our strategy revealed, I release Niklau's gaze. A second line of dragons, their leathery wings stretched wide and casting shadows over the soldiers running in a mad panic. As they swoop over the chaos, they pick off four more mages from among the soldiers. The dragons carry their prey to the sea and drop them far beyond the breaking point of the waves. It was the only way we could think of to dispose of the dust.

A third line of dragons coasts by, and four more blue-cloaked mages are plucked from the throng of confused soldiers. One mage manages to toss his green powder into the air. He catches most of the dust in his own face and immediately slumps in the dragon's clutch. Some settles on the soldiers below him, and they collapse where they stand.

The dragon—"Gero," Arik whispers in a gasp from behind me—catches powder in his snoot and comes down hard, though he lands on all four legs, crushing his self-poisoned captive beneath him.

This is why they couldn't weaponize their magically altered toxins. Humans are more susceptible to the poisons. In Niklau's arrogance, he'd been premature in his advance on the dracs. I shudder at the thought of his mages taking the time to create weapons that could properly target dragons.

The soldiers not killed by the toxin or crushed by the weight of him scatter.

Niklau raises his arms in outrage, but his screams are cut off by a final dragon who sweeps him off his horse and carries him off to the sea. We watch as the dragons form a circular flight pattern, ensuring the magically enhanced toxins disappear under the waves with the mages and Niklau.

The event lasts minutes, but the breathtaking majesty of a fleet of dragons soaring overhead and the lethal precision with which they snatch their targets will inspire awe for many lifetimes.

According to Devantdemar law, crimes are tried and judged by a council overseen by the king. But Arik and I agree that the crimes against the dracs are to be meted out by their clan. Vengeance is theirs.

Arik

The remaining dragons soar over the crowd, seeking out telltale blue robes. None emerge, and as much as I want them gone, I lament when we find none to hold for interrogation. But in the wake of the disbursing soldiers, dracs find three robes trampled into the ground, so our work is not finished.

Throughout the confrontation, I was tempted to transform into my dragon form and protect Ophelia, but we are not ready to reveal our shifter nature. Only Ophelia knows who we are. The only thing helping me keep my composure is her strength.

I gesture to two dracs and their riders to check on our fallen clanmate. One raises his hand to indicate he's okay. I nod to two more dracs. They know what to do. Our brother will not suffer the indignity of being gawked at. The two dragons grab their clanmate by fore and rear claws and carry him to the water's edge down shore where they can tend to him.

Arriving at the rear of the Penyasegat troops, Kerik heads the Devantdemar soldiers, which have emerged from the foothills in time to secure Niklau's army. In the absence of his leadership and ambitious directives, the soldiers lay down their weapons and mill around fearful and without purpose.

"Mercé," I order, "corral the Penyasegat soldiers and assist the chief marshal with their escort to the mountain passage and to their kingdom."

On her mate's back, Mercé organizes a small contingent of dragon keepers on dragonback to accompany the remaining Penyasegat force toward the mountains.

Ophelia's father emerges from the gates on horseback. I bury my face in her hair as Vix walks us forward to meet him.

"You should be the new chief marshal," her father calls out as he approaches. He may be joking, but the admiration is clear in his face.

I whisper for only her to hear. "Your role is queen."

She scoffs. "My father will live a long time to come."

"My queen. My drac queen."

"You had your chance to claim me once, but you lost it."

Her words punch a hole through my chest, and I blow out a hard breath.

"So I'm claiming you. You have no choice in the matter. I am your queen. We have a lot of rebuilding to do, but I love you."

Her body relaxes into mine enough for me to sense, but her posture is proud as her father meets us.

12

A Spring Feast

Arik

The doors of the great hall are open to the citizens of Devantdemar. Villagers and townsfolk meander the lower castle grounds, mingling and partaking of the entertainment, food, and drink available in and around the castle.

The grounds aren't large enough to accommodate all the kingdom's citizens during the Spring Feast, so celebrations spread along the perimeter road outside the castle walls. At various stations along the way, bonfires blaze, performers showcase their arts, merchants exhibit artisanal products, and vendors sell foods both exotic and familiar. Even the dragon keepers host a stall where drac adolescents in their dragon forms show off shiny scales, sharp claws, and leathery wings.

Although Ophelia and I agree to keep the secret of the drac shifting abilities, my kind are desperate to learn more about Ophelia's people. The same is true of her people. We compromise by permitting dragons and dracs as dragon keepers to visit Devantdemar, but no drac can shift within sight of the villages. Dracs come down from the peaks and shift only in the mountains, as we have done for these many years, thus our secret is still closely guarded. Dragon sightings are rare. It's a matter of time before the drac reveal themselves as shifters. After all, I revealed myself to my mate, a topic she and I would revisit later.

After the confrontation at the gates of the Devantdemar keep, the dracs surrounded the Penyasegat army and escorted them to the mountain passage. Without their king, rule falls to the king's privy council while they search for an heir.

Ophelia and I visited Penyasegat on dragonmount a few days later as Niklau's army arrived home. We were assured that the king's obsession with obtaining more magic was his own. Our drac spies are monitoring their evolution under council rule.

The princess's attendance at the festival consists of her walking the entire perimeter of the castle, stopping at each satellite spectacle. It's a day-long excursion in which she greets most likely every member of the Devantdemar citizenry with grace and enthusiasm.

All day, I hide my jealous impatience as townsfolk clutch her hands like old friends, thrust babies into her arms for quick cuddles, and share their personal dramas as though she were a favorite aunt. Her smile through it all is broad and genuine, and a light of contentment blazes in her eyes. I hope she saves some of that energy for me. I have plans for her.

We announce our betrothal at the day-long Spring Feast. She's made me wait to claim her until we've made a formal promise.

"It's a punishment for the torture of the two years I was gone from your life," I accuse with no little remorse.

But as a queen of her people, she's insistent. "We must include my people in the celebrations."

To that, I argue, "Mating is a private affair dracs share with no one."

She laughs at the claim. "We'll be mated before Fest de Verd, which we'll celebrate in a couple of weeks on the peaks with your dracs. Now, it's unseemly for a dragon chief to be so petulant."

She'll be a good leader for all our people. And the perfect mate for me.

By the time the sun settles on the mountaintops, we return to the great hall to join the dancing revelers. I threaten to sweep her away, but she extracts a promise of one dance from me before saying goodbye to her family for the day. She leaves me to change into her evening clothes.

Ophelia stands atop the stairs overlooking the great hall. Her dress is black and deep blue, and when she moves in the candlelight the beadwork shimmers like my scales. At the sight, my heart grows its own set of wings. The dress clings to her, hanging from two delicate straps. The neckline is just low enough to reveal the tops of her decadent breasts. The gown hugs her curves like a shimmering second skin until it reaches her hips and drapes freely to the ground. Wearing my colors, my dracmate steals my breath.

I wait at the bottom of the steps as she receives cheers from the guests crowded into the great hall. I sweep her through our dance distracted—I train all my focus on resisting the urge to run my hands all over her body in front of an audience.

Ophelia

My hands are bound behind me as I stand before him in my shimmering gown. He brought me back to the hot springs where two years ago we'd glimpsed the future we are now taking for ourselves.

"I planned to slash your dress off you, until I saw it," he says, running his hands along the elaborate fabric over my stomach.

"Don't you dare," I say. "I designed the beadwork to mirror your scales and coloring."

"I see that, my queen."

He stands before me naked, not having bothered with clothes when he shifted to human form after flying us to our spot.

He traces one strap of the dress, running the back of his finger over my collarbones and pulling at the delicate fabric. "I'd fuck you in it, but these beads wouldn't survive what I want to do to you."

He extends a claw and reaches around my back. He slashes the thin strap where it meets the dress, and I gasp. "Arik."

"That can be mended." He slashes the other strap. "That can too," he says with a smirk as the bodice falls to reveal my breasts.

He gently traces a ring around one nipple. The thrill of his sharp claw barely scraping my skin distracts me from feeling angry about my damaged dress.

He reaches around and tugs at the laces cinching the dress at my waist and loosens them enough to slide the garment over my hips and down my legs. He holds it so I can step out of it, then gingerly drapes it over a nearby rock.

I wear no undergarments. He stands back to enjoy the sight of me bare before him.

His eyes flash with an eagerness that sends a thrill through my body. Then he quirks a crooked smile.

"You've always been a good little princess, haven't you?"

"Yes, Chieftain."

He steps forward and cups my mound, slipping a finger into my folds.

"But now you're my queen. And queen to my people." He pats the inside of my thighs, and I step wide for him.

"I am, Chieftain."

"You're also a wicked little thing, aren't you?" He spanks my pussy.

I gasp, but my gaze never breaks from his. "You know I am," I say, panting.

"The mating requires two things, a bite with a taste of blood and good sound fucking."

"So ritualistic."

"You have a smart mouth for a chieftain's mate."

"I'm not your mate yet."

"That changes tonight," he says, gripping my hair to push me to my knees.

His rough treatment has my pussy throbbing. I keep my gaze fixed on his, and he strokes my jaw and throat with a claw.

"I'm going to bite you, and I'm going to draw blood. You're going to do the same."

"Arik, I won't be able to draw blood with my bite." I hear the concern in my own voice, but he bends a knee and brings my cheek to rest on his thigh.

"No. That's why we're doing this first. You take my blood now. Everything will fall into place when I bite you later."

He slices a small gash at the top of his thigh, near his groin, and presses my face against the cut. I have to nestle my face against his cock to lap up the blood, the cheeky dragon.

I kiss and lick the small wound. The moment I taste the salty, coppery blood, my throat contracts, my heart flutters, and a warmth floods my body. I feel small tremors in my pussy, orgasmic fluttering. I gasp and drop my head back. He groans and when our gazes meet, his eyes are black pools.

"Hmmm. You feel that," he says.

"Yes," I moan. "Now it's your turn."

"Not yet. First, I want my queen to suck my cock."

I don't hesitate. I open my mouth and present the flat of my tongue.

He releases a breathy chuckle. "You are my needy whore, aren't you?"

I nod with my mouth open. The thought of him using me makes me wetter. He doesn't tease me, slipping his cock into my mouth right away. He slides in and out a few times before pulling out of my mouth. I suck as he does.

"Naughty queen."

"Mhmm." I lick my lips before he slides in again, and my tongue strokes the underside of his thick dick.

I open my mouth as wide as I can for him to slide deeper. He pushes to the back of my throat, still gripping my hair. He moves back and forth slowly, allowing me to swallow each time he hits my throat, warming me up.

"You like it when I feed you my cock."

"Mhmm," I hum around him. He hisses in response.

"My fuck toy."

I hum again, and he thrusts deeper into my mouth, holding my head in place by my hair. He fucks my face with fast but measured strokes, keeping a rhythm I can breathe through. For the moment, at least.

"I love your filthy mouth. Such a good queen, taking my cock."

He thrusts deeper and faster. I close my eyes and relax my throat as I give myself over to him. He senses my surrender and begins fucking me in earnest. I gag around his cock, my pussy pulsing in anticipation with each thrust. He fucks my mouth as tears stream down my face. I willingly choke on my love's massive shaft. I inhale when I can, but otherwise he owns my entire existence, until he's pounding into me fast and erratic. Jets of cum hit the back of my throat. I try to swallow, but I choke out much of it as he finishes. It's messy, but he doesn't seem to mind as he rubs the cum and spit into my jaw and throat.

"Such a good cum whore, my queen."

Arik

She's devastating in her perfection. Time to claim her as mine. At last.

I pull out the bag of supplies I stowed behind a nearby rock earlier. I lay the blankets and furs out in front of her. Instead of changing her bindings to lay her on her back, I push her face into the blankets, her ass and cunt exposed to me.

She likes to be used like a fuck toy. I learned the pleasure she derives from rough fucking and hard use in the dungeons. I am designing our own dungeon, carved into the back of our suites, just for my queen's special punishments. And rewards.

I spank her ass once to remind her I'm there, then I lie down behind her and pull her over me to press my face into her cunt. There will be nothing romantic about this claiming. I lick her pussy and ass like a starved beast. She moans loud into the sky and shudders at the touch.

I'm anxious to mark my mate. I transform my mouth just enough to sharpen my teeth, and I bite down on her inner thigh. She screams, though not from pain. It's the snap that locks our psyches together, then the surge of lust that rips through both our bodies. As the wave crashes through us, she grinds her pussy against my face. I transform my human tongue into my dragon tongue, long and thick, and drive it into her cunt. My hips buck uncontrollably as she rides my face.

"Oh gods," she moans.

I want to tell her to use me, but I hold steady as her pussy drips honeyed juices down my throat. I wrap my arm around her and rub at her clit with fervor as she rides my face.

In moments, she's cumming around my tongue. I let her ride out her orgasm until she pulls off me and falls to her side atop the furs and blankets. But I don't let her get away. I turn her over and find her cunt again to lap at her juices and wipe her clean, as a good mate should.

I feel her satisfaction through our bond, as surely as she feels my need raging. The realization feeds her own need, and I can feel her hunger building again. I pull her ass back up into the air and plunge my cock into her.

"My queen," I say as I pound into her. "Tell me what you need."

"Fuck me, Arik. Use me 'til you break me."

Never, I think. *You're unbreakable.* I pound into her with the need of a man desperate to lay claim to the wife he almost lost. She feels my fear through our bond and sends me a reassurance that she's mine. My queen. My mate. My love. I fuck her hard, my pelvis slamming against her ass and my balls slapping against her clit. The lewd smacking of flesh against flesh echoes off the rock walls surrounding us. I hold back until I feel her on the cusp through our bond, her need pulling into a tightly wound coil. I redouble my pounding until she falls over the edge. I follow, cumming into her once again in rough, hard thrusts.

When I'm spent, I push us onto our sides, unfasten her bindings, and pull her limp body against mine. We feel our mutual exhaustion and satiation through our bond and revel in the sensation of our shared consciousness. We say nothing for a long time.

Ophelia

I hadn't expected the bond to be such an open conduit into his soul, but now that I'm there, I can't imagine not being connected to him. In time, the psychic link will become stronger and clearer, and someday we may communicate telepathically. But that's for a faraway future. For now, the sensation of pure and absolute love courses through our bond. I treasure my drac chieftain, my mate, my love.

ACKNOWLEDGMENTS

Thank you to my editor Lindsey Hinkel for her eagle eyes and keen insights, to my critique partners Emily Klein, Amy Prendergast, and Liann Zhang for their enthusiastic support and thoughtful attention, and to my beta readers Taylor Bullet, Jessie Quist, Melissa Rogers, Sigh, and Sofia Giaconda for their thoughtful and wise comments at various stages. It's a privilege to work with such talented writers and editors.

About Megan

Megan Landon is an Austin-based writer of erotic fantasy and sci-fi romance. Her intricately woven stories are inspired by nature, science, language, her Columbian and Dutch roots, her linguistic training, and magic. She writes intelligent heroines, supportive heroes, dark romance, and slightly off-center worlds. As a badass mother, daughter, wife, sister, scholar, and traveller who lives in the reality of the human condition, Meg admits losing oneself in fiction is the sport of literature. To that end, she loves a good damsel story. She especially loves to play with the shades of nuance that exist between light and dark, magic and reality, and truth and fiction. Megan Landon has a PhD in linguistics. Her erotic flash fiction has appeared in Bust Magazine, and she is a regular collaborator with the Erotica Consortium.

To receive updates about upcoming releases and get access to illustrations and related media, sign up for Meg's newsletter at www.meganlandon.com.